Max's Missing Mittens

Adventure

Eric Gale

Published by Lightwave Publishing, 2024.

This is a work of fiction. Similarities to real people, places, or events are entirely coincidental.

MAX'S MISSING MITTENS

First edition. November 18, 2024.

Copyright © 2024 Eric Gale.

ISBN: 979-8230999065

Written by Eric Gale.

Table of Contents

Preface 1
Chapter 1: The Mystery of the Missing Mittens Begins 2
Chapter 2: Patience with Tully 6
Chapter 3: The Organized Search with Rina 10
Chapter 4: Mistakes Happen with Boomer 14
Chapter 5: Perseverance with Una the Wise Owl 18
Chapter 6: Attention to Detail with Whisk the Fox 22
Chapter 7: Teamwork with Quinny the Hedgehog 26
Chapter 8: Responsibility with Sol the Sparrow 30
Chapter 9: Honesty with Mr. Ponder the Tortoise 34
Chapter 10: Positivity with Piper the Duckling 38
Chapter 11: Helping Others with Mrs. Mallow and the Marketplace 41
Chapter 12: Carefulness with Ollie the Otter 45
Chapter 13: Encouragement with Coach Bruno the Bear 49
Chapter 14: Listening and Wisdom with Grandma Hazel 52
Chapter 15: Problem-Solving with Finn the Squirrel 57
Chapter 16: Adaptability with Faye the Fox 61
Chapter 17: Resilience with Rocky the Badger 64
Chapter 18: Gratitude with Louie the Owl 68
Chapter 19: Empathy with Mira the Deer 71
Chapter 20: Patience in Reflection with Sage the Turtle 75
Chapter 21: Forgiveness with Ember the Crow 78
Chapter 22: Humility with Ezra the Snail 82
Chapter 23: Perseverance with Gia the Honeybee 86
Chapter 24: Honesty with Bosco the Hedgehog 89
Chapter 25: Reflection and Farewell at the Friendship Gathering 93

Preface

In writing *Max's Missing Mittens*, I hoped to create a story that would resonate with children, families, and anyone young at heart.

Max's adventure started with a simple quest to find his mittens, but it became a journey of discovering values and virtues that form the foundation of a fulfilling life. Each character Max meets is a reflection of the qualities we all aspire to embrace, and his journey is an invitation to approach life with patience, empathy, and resilience.

Through Max's story, I hope to remind readers that growth and learning are ongoing journeys. Every challenge, mistake, or small success adds to the tapestry of who we are becoming. This book is an invitation to explore and celebrate the journey of growth—one that begins with a small loss and ends in an invaluable discovery of friendship, gratitude, and self-discovery.

Chapter 1: The Mystery of the Missing Mittens Begins

The sun peeked through Max's bedroom window, casting a warm glow over his bed and waking him gently. Today was a special day—it was the first snowfall of the season, and Max had been waiting all week to wear his brand-new mittens to school. His mom had found them just for him, knitted in deep blue with little white snowflakes stitched along the cuffs. They were perfect.

Max got ready for school, brushing his teeth, combing his messy bed-head hair, and finally grabbing his backpack from the hook by the door. He called out, "Mom! Have you seen my mittens?" His mom poked her head around the corner with a smile.

"They're right where you left them last night, Max. Are you sure you'll keep track of them today? Remember, it's important to take care of your things, especially since you've been so excited about those mittens."

Max nodded enthusiastically, barely listening as he grabbed his mittens from the table by the door. He slid them on and admired how warm and cozy they felt, giving his fingers a little wiggle inside. "I'll take good care of them, promise!" he said, giving his mom a quick hug and dashing outside, where the snow crunched delightfully under his feet.

As Max walked to school, he admired the snow-covered trees and the soft way the world seemed to glow under its fresh, white blanket. He made a small snowball and tossed it up into the air, catching it in his mittened hands. The morning seemed perfect. But by the time he reached the schoolyard, Max's excitement had carried him through several snowball throws, a little jump across the snowy patch by the park, and even a tumble into a snow drift when he tried to race his friend Tully.

MAX'S MISSING MITTENS

"Max!" Tully, a slim, cheerful rabbit with a big smile and long ears, greeted him. "Want to play snow tag?"

Max grinned. "Absolutely! Just one round before the bell rings." They began chasing each other around, dodging in and out of snow piles, and laughing loudly as their breath turned to little puffs in the cold air. But as they ran, Max felt his hands getting colder and colder.

When he finally stopped to catch his breath, he looked down at his hands and gasped. His mittens were gone!

"Oh no, oh no, no, no!" Max muttered to himself, turning in frantic circles as he scanned the ground around him. "My mittens! Tully, I lost my new mittens!"

Tully's ears perked up, and his face softened as he saw Max's worried expression. "Don't worry, Max," he said with a reassuring smile. "We'll find them. Let's think this through. Where did you see them last?"

Max rubbed his hands together to warm them, his mind racing as he tried to remember. "I think... I had them on when I left the house. I was making snowballs, and I had them when we were playing... but I must have lost them while we were running around."

The bell rang, signaling the start of school, but Max felt uneasy the whole morning. His mind kept drifting back to his missing mittens. He could almost hear his mom's voice reminding him about taking care of his things, and the thought made his stomach twist. He'd promised her he would be responsible. Determined to make it right, Max decided that he would spend every bit of his break and lunch time searching until he found his mittens.

During recess, Max started looking along the path he had taken to school, with Tully by his side. "We'll retrace every step!" Tully said confidently. "Maybe they slipped off when you made that snowball."

Max nodded, and together they crouched down, scanning the snow-covered ground. They checked around the playground swings, behind the slide, and even under the benches where some of the kids would sit to tie their boots. But his mittens were nowhere to be found.

"Maybe they blew away?" Tully wondered aloud, looking around at the trees that lined the edge of the playground.

Max bit his lip, feeling a pang of guilt. He knew he should have paid more attention. "They were my favorite mittens, Tully. I feel terrible about losing them, and I didn't even have them for one full day!"

Tully patted Max on the shoulder with a comforting smile. "It's okay, Max. Sometimes things get lost. We'll keep looking, and if we don't find them today, we'll keep looking tomorrow too."

They spent every spare moment searching—first around the school, then outside along the sidewalks and under the trees. By the time the final bell rang at the end of the school day, Max was no closer to finding his mittens than he had been in the morning. Despite his best efforts, his hands were still bare, and his heart felt heavy with disappointment.

As he walked home, Max couldn't help but feel like he'd let himself down. Maybe he hadn't been as responsible as he'd thought. He'd promised his mom he would take care of his mittens, but he'd allowed himself to get so distracted with fun that he forgot to check for them. His head hung low as he trudged through the snow, trying to figure out what he would say to his mom.

When he reached home, Max slowly took off his boots and coat, dreading the moment he would have to tell his mom about his lost mittens. She appeared in the doorway with a warm smile, which quickly faded when she noticed his empty hands.

"Max, where are your mittens?"

Max took a deep breath, deciding that he had to be honest, even if it felt hard. "Mom, I lost them. I didn't mean to. I tried really hard to look for them, but they were just gone. I think I lost them while I was playing snow tag."

His mom looked at him kindly, kneeling down so that they were at eye level. "Thank you for telling me the truth, Max. I know it's disappointing to lose something important, but I'm proud of you for trying your best to find them and for being honest about it."

Max nodded, feeling a little better, but the disappointment lingered. "I'll keep looking tomorrow," he said, determined. "And I promise, next time, I'll be extra careful with my things."

His mom gave him a hug and ruffled his hair. "That's a good plan, Max. Being responsible means learning from mistakes, not just getting everything right all the time. Let's talk tonight about how you can remember to keep track of your things."

Max climbed into bed that night with a small smile, thinking about his mom's words. Maybe he hadn't been as careful as he should have, but tomorrow was another day. And he wasn't alone—he had Tully and his friends to help him, too. Max drifted off to sleep with a hopeful heart, ready to begin his search again.

Chapter 2: Patience with Tully

The next morning, Max woke up determined. He was going to find his mittens, no matter what. His mom had packed him an extra pair of gloves to wear while he searched, but Max promised himself that by the end of the day, he'd have his blue mittens back on his hands.

At school, Max met Tully by the big tree near the playground. Tully, the friendly rabbit, was waiting for him with a warm smile and a hop in his step. "Are you ready, Max?" Tully asked, wiggling his long ears with excitement. "Today, we're going to find those mittens, I just know it!"

Max nodded, feeling a renewed sense of hope. "Thanks for helping me again, Tully. I don't know what I'd do without you."

"No worries," Tully replied cheerfully. "Friends help each other, right? Besides, this is like a big adventure! We'll just have to be very patient and look in all the right places."

Max's shoulders relaxed as he realized that he wasn't alone in his search. Having Tully by his side made him feel much more confident. They set off toward the playground, where they'd played tag the day before.

The playground was bustling with activity. Kids were climbing on the jungle gym, swinging high in the air, and sliding down the frosty slide. Max's eyes darted around, hoping to spot a flash of blue against the white snow, but so far, he didn't see his mittens anywhere.

"Let's check under the benches and around the swings," Tully suggested. "Sometimes, things fall in hidden spots, and it takes a little patience to find them."

Max and Tully crouched down, peering under each bench and combing through the snow around the swing set. They moved slowly, making sure not to miss a single spot. Each time Max thought he saw a bit of blue, it would turn out to be a wrapper, a fallen piece of paper, or even a tiny pebble.

After searching for a while, Max started feeling a little frustrated. "It's so hard to wait and look so carefully," he muttered, feeling his patience wearing thin. "What if we never find them, Tully?"

Tully smiled softly, patting Max on the shoulder. "Sometimes, things take longer than we expect, but that doesn't mean they aren't possible," he said. "Patience is just another part of finding what's important to you. Besides, we're making progress!"

Max sighed but nodded. Tully was right. If he gave up now, he'd never find his mittens, and he'd feel even worse. Taking a deep breath, Max decided to push through his impatience and keep looking.

Next, they decided to check around the slide, where they'd been playing the day before. The area was covered in small footprints, so they had to look even more carefully. Max remembered how he'd tossed a few snowballs in the air while playing with Tully, so he tried to imagine exactly where he might have lost his mittens.

"Hey, Tully," Max said, squinting his eyes to retrace their steps. "Maybe we should go back over to the snow drift near the park. That's where we were playing the longest yesterday."

"Great idea, Max!" Tully replied, bouncing up and down with enthusiasm. "Thinking back to what we did might give us some clues. Let's go over and check it out!"

Together, they walked over to the large snow drift near the park's entrance. It was the tallest snow pile on the playground, big enough that some kids had built tiny tunnels and forts into its sides. Max and Tully approached carefully, noticing the small caves kids had dug out for their imaginary games.

"Do you remember if you fell in here, or if maybe you dropped something while making snowballs?" Tully asked, gently prodding the snow with his paw.

Max thought back to yesterday, trying to remember if he'd done anything that could have led to him dropping his mittens. "I... I remember making a really big snowball here and tossing it up really high," Max said slowly, piecing together his memories. "Maybe one of my mittens fell off when I threw it."

With renewed hope, the two friends began digging gently into the snow drift, checking inside each little tunnel and around the edges. They worked slowly, trying to be as thorough as possible. Max noticed that while he was digging, his frustration from earlier was fading. The search felt almost calming as he focused on the task at hand.

After a while, Max sat back on his heels and looked at Tully, who was carefully inspecting the side of the drift. "You know, Tully," Max said thoughtfully, "I'm starting to understand what you meant about patience. It's like, the more time we take, the better chance we have of finding them."

Tully nodded, his eyes twinkling. "Exactly! Rushing only makes it harder to notice important details. When we're patient, we're more likely to spot what we're looking for."

Just then, Tully spotted something small and blue peeking out from a patch of snow at the far end of the drift. "Max! Look over here!" he shouted, waving Max over.

Max's heart leaped as he ran to Tully's side, only to realize that the blue object was a small, forgotten toy left by another child. His heart sank for a moment, but he quickly reminded himself of what Tully had said. They'd just have to keep looking, and it would take the time it took.

They continued their search, moving slowly and thoroughly around each part of the playground and checking every spot where they might find a clue. Max began to notice small things he'd missed before, like the way the snow had settled in layers or how tiny, colorful objects could stand out against the white snow.

Finally, the school bell rang, calling them back to class. Though Max hadn't found his mittens, he felt a sense of accomplishment. He'd spent the whole morning being patient, and it had taught him something valuable. Tully walked alongside him, his calm presence helping Max stay positive.

Chapter 3: The Organized Search with Rina

The next morning, Max headed to school with a fresh resolve. Today, he was determined to find his mittens. He'd learned from Tully that patience was essential, but he couldn't shake the feeling that maybe he could approach the search in a different way. When he reached the schoolyard, he spotted Tully talking with their friend Rina by the swing set.

Rina, a clever and meticulous squirrel, always had a plan for everything. She was known for her love of organizing and was never seen without her tiny notebook where she jotted down important ideas. Seeing her, Max felt a spark of hope. If anyone could help him search with a new strategy, it was Rina.

"Good morning, Max!" Rina greeted him, noticing his glum expression. "Any luck with the mittens?"

Max shook his head. "Not yet. Tully and I searched all over the playground yesterday, but we didn't find anything." He sighed. "I was patient, like Tully said, but maybe I'm just not looking in the right way."

Rina nodded thoughtfully, adjusting her tiny notebook in her paws. "Well, maybe we need a more organized plan. A good search often starts with careful thinking and a bit of a checklist. Why don't we try making a list of all the places you might have been?"

Max's face brightened as he realized Rina's method might help him remember something he'd overlooked. "That sounds like a great idea, Rina! Let's do it."

The three friends sat down on a bench, and Rina opened her notebook. She quickly drew three columns and labeled them "Location," "What We Did," and "Checked Already?" She looked up at Max with an encouraging smile.

"Okay, Max, think back to everywhere you went yesterday," she prompted, pencil poised and ready to write.

Max scratched his head, trying to recall every detail. "Well, I started at home, and then I walked here. On the way, I made some snowballs by the park. Then, Tully and I played tag all over the playground."

Rina nodded, noting each location. "Good start! That gives us the house, the park, and the playground as places to check carefully. Now, let's mark whether we've already searched those areas."

Max and Tully chimed in together. "We already checked the playground yesterday."

Rina marked the "playground" row as "checked" but kept it on the list. "Just because we checked once doesn't mean we can't find something new today. Now, where else might you have gone?"

Max thought hard, recalling as many details as possible. "After school, I walked home, but I stopped by the corner where Mrs. Willow has her big garden. I was looking at the snow covering her flowers."

Rina scribbled "Mrs. Willow's Garden" in the notebook and made a small star next to it. "We can check there on our way home. Maybe something slipped off there, especially if you were reaching down to look at the flowers."

Max's confidence grew with each new place added to their list. He realized that Rina's method was helping him remember small details he'd forgotten.

Their first stop was the park, where Max had been making snowballs. They combed through the bushes and searched around the benches, but there was no sign of the mittens. Max felt his heart sink a little, but Rina was quick to remind him that their list had several other places to try.

"Searching takes time, but each place we check gets us closer," she said with a determined nod. "Next stop: Mrs. Willow's Garden."

As they walked over, Tully looked at Rina with admiration. "You're so organized, Rina. It's really helpful! I never would have thought to make a list like this."

Rina shrugged, smiling modestly. "It's just my way of thinking. When I have a problem, organizing everything helps me feel more in control. I think it can be useful for anyone, especially for tricky situations like this."

Mrs. Willow's garden, though blanketed in snow, looked beautiful. Her hedges were delicately covered in frost, and the tall birch trees around her yard cast long shadows over the soft, white ground. Max led the way as the trio began looking around the garden's edge, near where he'd knelt to inspect the snow-covered flowers.

"Anything yet?" Max asked, peering into the bushes.

Tully shook his head, sifting through the snow with his paws. "Nothing yet, but I'm sure we'll find something soon!"

Rina was deep in thought, looking at the pathway that led through the garden and back toward the road. "Max, did you maybe walk down the pathway? It's easy to drop something when you're moving."

Max nodded. "I think so. I remember looking around a lot, so maybe one of my mittens slipped off."

With this new angle, they searched along the pathway, looking carefully where footprints had pressed the snow flat. After a while, though, it became clear that the mittens weren't there either. Rina checked off Mrs. Willow's garden on her list, marking it with a small "X."

Their next stop was the library. Rina remembered Max saying that he'd briefly stopped there to say hello to their teacher, who was volunteering. They checked the coat rack and all around the entrance, even peeking under the tables and chairs in case Max had set his mittens down. But after a thorough search, they still didn't find anything.

Max slumped his shoulders, feeling the weight of disappointment once again. "It's like they just disappeared into thin air."

Rina closed her notebook, patting him on the shoulder with an understanding smile. "Sometimes, things don't show up right away, even if we try our best. But with each place we check, we're getting closer to figuring out where they might be. The important part is that we don't give up."

Tully replied, "Exactly, Max! Every search is a step closer. And hey, we've covered a lot of ground today thanks to Rina's plan."

Chapter 4: Mistakes Happen with Boomer

The following day, Max was ready with his list in hand, prepared to continue his mitten search. His mom had given him a hug before he left, telling him she was proud of his determination. But as he approached the playground, Max saw someone he hadn't seen in a while—Boomer, the big, friendly raccoon. Boomer was known for being a bit clumsy, but he always had a cheerful grin and a heart as big as the playground itself.

Boomer waved, his eyes lighting up when he saw Max and Tully. "Hey there, Max! Heard you lost your mittens. That's a real bummer, buddy."

Max smiled back, feeling comforted by Boomer's kindness. "Yeah, I did. I've been looking everywhere. Tully and Rina have been helping me, but no luck yet."

Boomer's ears perked up, and he gave Max a hearty pat on the shoulder, almost knocking him off balance. "Don't you worry, Max! I'll help too. I know all about losing things. Happens to me all the time. Just last week, I misplaced my lunch three times before I found it tucked under my own tail!"

Max chuckled, feeling a little lighter. Boomer's enthusiasm and honesty about his own mistakes were somehow comforting. Max thought that maybe Boomer's experience with losing things would be useful. Plus, Boomer was great at looking in all the odd places no one else thought of.

They started their search near the back of the school building, where Boomer insisted there might be "secret mitten hiding spots." Max and Tully followed him, laughing as he dug into piles of leaves, peeked behind tree trunks, and even looked up in the branches as if his mittens might have floated there.

14

"You know, Max," Boomer said as he lifted up a pile of leaves, "I've lost my backpack, my scarf, and even my favorite hat this way. My mom says it's because I don't pay enough attention to where I put things."

Max tilted his head thoughtfully. "Maybe that's what happened to me too. I was playing tag and not paying much attention to my mittens. They just slipped away without me noticing."

Boomer grinned, brushing the leaves off his paws. "See? Sometimes it's not that we're careless, just that we're having so much fun that we forget! But it's okay, everyone makes mistakes. What matters is that we try to fix them, right?"

Max nodded, encouraged by Boomer's positive attitude. Boomer wasn't embarrassed about his mistakes; instead, he used them as an opportunity to learn and laugh about it. Inspired, Max decided he wouldn't feel bad about his lost mittens but would instead focus on doing his best to find them.

The trio continued their search around the back of the school, with Boomer leading them through places Max and Tully hadn't thought to check. At one point, Boomer slipped on a patch of ice and tumbled into a snowbank, sending up a flurry of snow. Max and Tully couldn't help but laugh as Boomer emerged, shaking the snow off with a grin.

"No mittens here!" Boomer announced, chuckling. "But hey, you never know unless you look!"

Max realized that Boomer's approach—looking everywhere without worry—was surprisingly helpful. It reminded him not to get too hung up on any one place but to keep an open mind about where his mittens might have ended up. Boomer's fun-loving attitude made the search feel less like a chore and more like an adventure.

After a while, they moved to the school's storage shed, a small wooden structure at the edge of the playground where the school kept sports equipment and other supplies. Boomer, with his adventurous spirit, suggested they peek inside in case Max had been nearby during recess and left his mittens there.

"I remember walking by the shed," Max said, thinking back. "I didn't go inside, but maybe I was close enough that they fell near the door."

The shed was locked, but they could still check around the outside. The three friends circled the shed, peering under benches and checking behind bins, searching for any sign of Max's mittens. Boomer even checked the tops of the bins in case someone had picked up the mittens and placed them there.

As they moved along, Boomer tripped over a rock and almost sent himself toppling into the snow again. He steadied himself, laughing heartily. "Oops! There I go again, tripping over my own paws."

Max laughed, feeling grateful for Boomer's ability to find humor in any situation. "Boomer, you're amazing. I'd be so frustrated if I kept tripping, but you just keep going and laughing."

Boomer shrugged, flashing a toothy grin. "You know, Max, if you get too upset every time you make a mistake, you'd never get anything done. I just think, 'Oh well!' and keep going. That way, I don't feel so bad, and I always remember to keep trying."

Max took Boomer's words to heart. Boomer was teaching him that sometimes, mistakes happen, but they don't have to ruin your day. Instead of feeling down, you could keep smiling, learn from them, and keep moving forward.

After the shed, they decided to check the area near the slide again, just in case they'd missed something the first time. As they walked, Boomer told Max stories about his clumsiest moments, each one funnier than the last. From forgetting his own snack under a tree to misplacing his rain boots inside his mother's closet, Boomer's stories were endless.

By the time they reached the slide, Max was laughing so hard his sides hurt. "Boomer, I think you've taught me that it's okay to make mistakes. I was so worried about losing my mittens because I promised my mom I'd take care of them, but you've shown me that sometimes things just happen."

Boomer nodded sagely, placing a paw on Max's shoulder. "Exactly, Max! It's great to be careful and keep your promises, but if something goes wrong, just remember to keep trying your best. Mistakes are just part of learning."

Tully, who'd been listening with a smile, chimed in. "You know, Boomer's right, Max. None of us are perfect, and losing things now and then doesn't make you any less responsible. It just means you're learning like everyone else."

Max felt a sense of relief as he listened to his friends. He realized that he'd been so focused on feeling guilty about losing the mittens that he hadn't stopped to appreciate his efforts to find them. Thanks to Boomer, he now understood that making mistakes didn't define him; what mattered was how he handled them afterward.

They continued searching near the slide, but by the end of the day, the mittens were still missing. However, instead of feeling disappointed, Max felt a sense of peace. Boomer had shown him that mistakes were okay and that his friends supported him, no matter what. With each search, he was learning more than just how to find lost mittens—he was discovering how to be kinder to himself.

Chapter 5: Perseverance with Una the Wise Owl

The next day, Max was back at school, feeling more determined than ever. His patience with Tully and his newfound understanding from Boomer had given him the motivation to keep trying, but he still hadn't found his mittens. As Max sat on a bench during recess, thinking about where to search next, he heard a soft, familiar "hoo" from above.

Looking up, he saw Una, the wise old owl, perched on a branch in the schoolyard's biggest tree. Una was known for her gentle, thoughtful ways, and many of the younger animals looked up to her. Max had often listened to her stories about life and the lessons she'd learned, so he felt a sense of relief when he saw her there, as though she might have the guidance he needed.

"Good morning, Max," Una said in her calm, soft voice. She tilted her head to look at him closely with her wise, golden eyes. "You look troubled. Is something bothering you?"

Max nodded, feeling a sense of comfort in Una's presence. "I lost my mittens a few days ago, Una. They were new, and I promised my mom I'd take care of them. I've searched with my friends every day, but I still haven't found them."

Una hooted softly, her eyes twinkling with understanding. "It sounds like you've been trying hard, Max. But tell me, do you feel like giving up?"

Max thought about it for a moment. He did feel tired, and part of him was frustrated that he hadn't found his mittens yet. But at the same time, he didn't want to give up. He wanted to keep trying until he found them, no matter how long it took.

"I do feel tired, but I don't want to stop searching," Max admitted, looking up at Una. "I just wish I knew how to keep going when it feels so hard."

Una nodded, folding her wings neatly as she perched. "Perseverance is a special quality, Max. It means continuing on, even when the journey is difficult. Sometimes, what we're looking for isn't found right away, but that doesn't mean it's lost forever. Perhaps it's hiding just around the corner, waiting for you to try one more time."

Max listened closely, feeling encouraged by Una's words. Her calmness made the search feel less urgent, as though he could keep trying a little longer without feeling so pressured.

"Would you help me search today, Una?" he asked, hoping her wisdom would help guide him in his efforts.

Una smiled, her golden eyes warm with kindness. "I'd be glad to help, Max. Let's begin by thinking carefully about where you might have missed. A thoughtful search can often reveal things we wouldn't expect."

The two of them walked together to the edge of the playground, where Max had searched with Tully and Boomer. Una moved slowly, inspecting each area with a careful eye, encouraging Max to do the same.

"Remember, sometimes what we seek is hidden in plain sight," Una said, guiding Max toward the snowy bushes at the playground's edge. "Looking slowly and carefully can be just as important as looking everywhere."

Max crouched down, moving the branches aside and examining each part of the bushes. He had looked here before with Tully, but this time, he tried to move more slowly, scanning every inch as he went. Though he didn't see his mittens, he felt that Una's advice was helping him feel more focused, less hurried. It was as if he could see everything more clearly by simply moving slowly and not rushing to the next place.

"Sometimes, when we're too focused on finding something, we miss the small things that lead us there," Una said, nodding at Max's careful inspection of the bushes. "By learning patience and taking our time, we can see more clearly."

As they continued, Max started to realize that part of his frustration had come from feeling like he needed to find his mittens right away. With Una's calm approach, though, the pressure seemed to lift, and he found himself feeling grateful for the journey itself. Searching with friends and learning from them had been special, and he realized he didn't want to give up—not because he was determined to win, but because he enjoyed the journey.

Next, they moved over to the big oak tree near the edge of the schoolyard, where Max remembered climbing earlier in the week. Una perched on one of the lower branches, her wise gaze sweeping the ground.

"Tell me, Max," Una asked as she scanned the area, "What have you learned from all your searching?"

Max thought back over the past few days. "I've learned about patience from Tully, and Boomer taught me not to worry about mistakes so much. Rina showed me how to organize my search, and now you're teaching me about perseverance. I guess… I've learned that each friend has something unique to share with me."

Una hooted softly, pleased with his answer. "That's right, Max. And each of those lessons you've learned is like a piece of a puzzle. Together, they make a complete picture of what it means to be resilient, to keep trying even when things are difficult."

As Max and Una continued their search, they approached the fence on the other side of the yard. Una's eyes swept across the snow, her vision sharp and clear.

"Perseverance doesn't just mean keeping on with a task," Una said. "It also means finding strength in your journey, in the friends who help you, and in the lessons you learn. Whether you find your mittens or not, Max, you'll come away with more than you started with."

Max felt a swell of gratitude for his wise friend. He hadn't found his mittens yet, but he'd gained something even more valuable—patience, determination, and the willingness to keep going. With each lesson, he felt himself growing stronger, becoming someone who could handle life's little challenges more calmly.

They finished their search around the schoolyard, but the mittens were still missing. Max turned to Una, smiling despite his lack of success. "Thank you, Una. I didn't find my mittens, but I feel... different. Like I've learned something more important."

Chapter 6: Attention to Detail with Whisk the Fox

On the morning of the sixth day, Max was ready with a new sense of purpose, driven by the lessons he had learned from his friends. Today, he hoped to bring an even sharper focus to his search. As he stood at the edge of the schoolyard, he saw Whisk, a sleek, bright-eyed fox with a reputation for spotting even the tiniest details. Whisk was known as the keenest observer around, often noticing things others overlooked.

Max waved to Whisk, and the fox trotted over with an alert look in his eyes. "Max! I heard about your missing mittens. How's the search going?"

Max sighed, though he was determined to stay positive. "I've looked everywhere, Whisk, and each day my friends help me in a new way. But I still haven't found them."

Whisk cocked his head thoughtfully. "Maybe it's time to look with a different kind of focus. Sometimes, the smallest details hold the biggest clues. Would you like me to join you?"

Max's face lit up. "Yes, please! I could really use your help, Whisk. You always seem to notice things that other people don't."

With Whisk's offer, they set off toward the playground, where Max had been playing tag the day he lost his mittens. As they walked, Whisk explained his way of seeing things. "The trick, Max, is not just to look around, but to look closely. Details often hide in plain sight, blending into the background, but if you learn to spot them, you can discover things you never noticed before."

Max listened closely, eager to learn from Whisk's sharp sense of observation. As they arrived at the playground, Whisk immediately began scanning the area with a careful, methodical gaze, his eyes sweeping every corner and crevice.

MAX'S MISSING MITTENS 23

They started near the swings, where Max had run around with Tully. Whisk pointed out a few small things Max had missed on previous searches—a scrap of paper half-buried in the snow, a colorful button lost by someone else, even a tiny ribbon frozen into the ground.

"You see, Max," Whisk said, flicking his tail as he looked at each small item, "not everything we find will be what we're looking for, but noticing these details is part of learning to observe. It helps us train our eyes."

Max nodded, crouching beside Whisk and observing each tiny object they found. Although these things weren't his mittens, Max began to feel a sense of accomplishment just by noticing more. He felt as if his view of the playground was sharper, more vibrant, and that he could see things in a new way.

After carefully combing through the area around the swings, Whisk led them over to the snowy bushes by the side of the playground. "Let's check here," Whisk suggested, his eyes narrowing as he scanned the tangled branches.

Max remembered how he'd looked here before with Una and Boomer, but he followed Whisk's advice and took a deep breath, focusing on every detail he could see. Together, they peered under each branch, looked through the snow, and even inspected the leaves that clung to the bushes.

Suddenly, Whisk paused, tilting his head toward a small indentation in the snow. "Look here, Max," he whispered. "It's a tiny pawprint. Much smaller than mine or Tully's."

Max squinted at the pawprint and realized it was something he'd never noticed before. "You're right, Whisk! I didn't even see that. Do you think it's a clue?"

Whisk nodded, his eyes glinting with excitement. "It could be. Maybe another animal found your mitten and took it with them. If we follow these tracks, we might find a hint of where it went."

Max's heart raced as they carefully followed the pawprints, which led away from the playground and toward the far side of the school. The tracks weaved in and out of small bushes and finally disappeared by a tree near the fence.

Though they didn't find the mittens, the trail gave Max a surge of hope. Following the small pawprints had shown him that even the tiniest details could lead to something valuable. And with Whisk's help, he was starting to see things he'd missed before.

After the playground, Whisk suggested they check along the path that led to the school entrance. "Let's look closely at the edges of the pathway," he said. "Sometimes, things slip to the side and are easy to overlook."

They slowly walked down the path, eyes scanning the ground on either side. Max spotted tiny objects—another piece of ribbon, a crumpled note, and even a shiny pebble that glittered in the sunlight. Though these weren't his mittens, he felt a thrill each time he noticed something new, his eyes sharpening with every step.

When they reached the front of the school, Whisk turned to Max with an approving look. "You're getting much better at spotting details, Max. It takes practice, but soon, you'll be able to see things more clearly every time you look."

Max grinned, feeling proud of his progress. "Thanks, Whisk. I never realized there was so much to see! Even though I didn't find my mittens yet, I feel like I'm really learning something important."

Whisk smiled, pleased to see Max's excitement. "Remember, Max, even if we don't find what we're looking for, we can always learn something valuable along the way. Observing carefully helps us understand the world better and notice things we might need later."

Max nodded, feeling a new sense of confidence. They decided to check one more place before the end of recess: the big oak tree near the back of the playground. As they walked, Max focused on everything around him, looking at each small patch of snow, each leaf, and each shadow with newfound curiosity.

When they reached the oak tree, Whisk suggested they inspect the roots, where many small animals often hid things. Max crouched down and looked closely at the twisted roots, moving carefully as he examined each nook and cranny. Even though his mittens weren't there, Max was fascinated by the small pieces of nature he found—tiny sticks, a couple of acorns, and even a feather stuck between two roots.

Chapter 7: Teamwork with Quinny the Hedgehog

The next day, Max arrived at school feeling more encouraged than ever. He had learned patience, perseverance, and even the art of observation, but today he had a feeling he would need something more. As he made his way across the playground, he spotted Quinny, a small but energetic hedgehog with a quick mind and a love for helping others. Quinny was well-known for her problem-solving skills, and she always brought a sense of optimism to every challenge.

Max smiled and waved as he approached her. "Hey, Quinny! I've been searching everywhere for my mittens, and I still can't find them. I could really use some help today."

Quinny's face lit up, her tiny nose twitching with excitement. "I'd love to help, Max! Sometimes it just takes a fresh pair of eyes and a bit of teamwork to solve a mystery like this. Let's team up and see what we can accomplish together!"

Max felt a surge of hope. He knew Quinny's cheerful spirit and clever thinking might be just what he needed. With Quinny's help, they might approach the search in a new way that he hadn't tried before.

Quinny led Max over to a quiet corner of the playground, away from the other students. "Let's start by planning out where we'll search," she suggested. "Good teamwork always starts with a clear plan so everyone knows what they need to do."

Max nodded, eager to follow her lead. "What do you think we should do first?"

Quinny tapped her chin thoughtfully, her small quills bristling with enthusiasm. "How about we divide up the playground into sections? We can each take a section and search it thoroughly. Then we'll meet back here to compare notes and see if either of us finds anything."

Max agreed, and they quickly divided the playground into sections: Max would search around the swings and the nearby snowbanks, while Quinny would cover the jungle gym and the open field. They gave each other a high-five and set off to their respective areas, both determined to look as carefully as possible.

Max began his search, remembering what Whisk had taught him about looking for small details. He crouched down by the snowbank, moving his hands through the snow to feel for anything that might be hidden beneath the surface. He felt a few twigs and pebbles, but no mittens. Still, he didn't feel discouraged. Knowing Quinny was also searching gave him a sense of motivation and hope.

Meanwhile, Quinny was combing through the area around the jungle gym. Her small size allowed her to squeeze between the bars and check all the hidden nooks and crannies. As she searched, she thought about other times she'd worked with friends to solve problems. Each time, she'd learned something new about how teamwork could make difficult tasks feel easier.

After a thorough search of their sections, Max and Quinny met back at their starting point to share what they'd found. Max hadn't found his mittens, but he had noticed some familiar footprints that he thought might lead to a clue. Quinny had come across a few more small objects left by other students, but nothing that looked like Max's mittens.

"Okay, so no mittens yet," Quinny said, "but maybe we need to expand our search. How about we work together on each section and combine our strengths? That way, we can double-check each area and make sure we don't miss anything."

Max agreed, realizing that their combined efforts could be even more effective. "Great idea, Quinny! Let's start with the jungle gym since you already looked there once."

They made their way over to the jungle gym, this time working side by side. Quinny pointed out places she'd already checked, and Max added his own observations. Together, they double-checked the space, moving slowly and making sure they didn't miss a single corner.

As they worked, Max noticed how Quinny's approach complemented his own. Quinny was quick to spot unusual patterns, like how the snow seemed a little more pressed down in one spot, while Max was careful to look under every bar and around each crevice. Their combined methods made the search feel more thorough and organized.

They moved to the open field next, where Max had played tag earlier in the week. This area was much larger, so they decided to split up again but stayed close enough that they could see each other. They both scanned the field, looking for any sign of the blue mittens against the white snow.

Quinny suddenly called out, "Max, come look at this!" She pointed to a small indentation in the snow near the edge of the field. It wasn't a mitten, but it was something that looked like a path, as though something had been dragged across the snow.

Max hurried over, his heart racing with excitement. "Do you think it could be from my mittens?"

Quinny inspected the trail closely, her eyes narrowing with focus. "It's possible. Let's follow it and see where it leads."

They walked carefully along the trail, which curved around the edge of the field and led toward a small cluster of trees. Max's excitement grew with each step. The trail ended near the base of one of the trees, where they found a small burrow in the snow, half-covered with twigs.

Max crouched down, peering into the burrow. Inside, he saw a few bits of leaves, some small rocks, and a tuft of fur—but no mittens. He sighed, feeling a mixture of disappointment and curiosity. The trail had been a promising lead, but it hadn't led to his mittens.

Quinny patted him on the shoulder. "Don't feel bad, Max. Following clues is part of the process, even if they don't always lead to what we're looking for. Each clue brings us closer to understanding where we might look next."

Max nodded, grateful for Quinny's optimism. Together, they moved on from the burrow and decided to check one last area: the benches near the school entrance. This time, they worked as a team from the beginning, each taking a bench and checking under, around, and behind it.

As they searched, Quinny shared stories about other times she'd solved problems with friends. "One time, my friend Daisy lost her hat, and it was only by working together that we found it. We each had our own ideas, but when we combined them, we came up with a plan that worked even better."

Max listened, inspired by Quinny's stories of teamwork. He realized that he'd been learning something valuable with each friend he'd worked with, and each of their unique skills had brought him closer to finding his mittens.

Finally, the recess bell rang, signaling the end of their search for the day. Quinny turned to Max with a smile. "Even though we didn't find your mittens today, I think we made great progress. You're a great teammate, Max."

Chapter 8: Responsibility with Sol the Sparrow

Max was starting to feel that each day brought him a new lesson in his search for his missing mittens. After learning about patience, perseverance, and teamwork, he was determined to find his mittens by becoming even more responsible. So, on the eighth day of his search, he sought out Sol, a wise sparrow known for his calm, thoughtful nature and his keen sense of responsibility.

Sol was perched on a branch near the school entrance, fluffed up against the chilly morning air. Max waved and called up to him, "Good morning, Sol! I was hoping you could help me with my search today."

Sol tilted his head, his bright eyes focused on Max with a gentle curiosity. "Hello, Max. I'd be happy to help you. I've heard about your missing mittens. It sounds like you've already been working hard to find them."

Max nodded, feeling a surge of determination. "Yes, I've looked everywhere, and my friends have all taught me new ways to search. But I think I might need to focus more on being responsible if I want to find them. Can you help me with that?"

Sol hopped down to a lower branch, closer to Max's eye level. "Responsibility is an important lesson, Max. It's not just about searching; it's about taking care of things, remembering where we place them, and learning from the experience. Sometimes, when we take responsibility for our actions, we discover new ways to approach a problem."

Max thought about this, realizing that he hadn't thought much about where he could have left his mittens. His friends had all been so helpful, but he hadn't spent much time retracing his own steps in detail. With Sol's help, he felt ready to take a more active role in his search.

MAX'S MISSING MITTENS

They began their search near the school entrance, where Max often placed his backpack before recess. Sol fluttered down from his branch and stood beside Max, guiding him to think carefully.

"Now, Max," Sol said, his voice calm and wise, "when was the last time you remember having your mittens, exactly? Think back to the moment you felt them on your hands. Responsibility starts with remembering the little details about where we were and what we were doing."

Max took a deep breath and closed his eyes, trying to remember the exact sequence of events. "I remember I was playing tag with Tully. I was wearing my mittens when we started, but I got distracted with the game. I think I tossed a snowball, and maybe one of my mittens slipped off around that time."

Sol nodded approvingly. "Good, Max. Now, retracing your steps with that memory in mind will make the search more focused. Let's start at the playground and look carefully along the path you took when you were playing."

Max led Sol to the area near the swings where he and Tully had started their game. This time, instead of simply scanning the area, he tried to recall each part of his movement: where he'd thrown the snowball, where he'd run, and where he might have tugged at his mittens to adjust them.

Sol watched with a wise eye, occasionally offering gentle suggestions. "Think about the little moments, Max. Did you take your mittens off for any reason? Or perhaps shake them out if snow got inside?"

Max paused, remembering that he had indeed pulled off his mittens briefly to shake out some snow. He realized he might have dropped them right then, without even noticing. He knelt down, checking the snow more carefully around the spot where he remembered stopping.

As he scanned the ground, he found small objects hidden in the snow—a shiny button, a bit of ribbon from another child's coat, even a pebble that looked like a tiny heart. Although he didn't find his mittens, the focused search made him feel more in control, as though he was finally taking true responsibility for finding them.

Next, they moved to the area near the slide, another spot where Max had played that day. Sol encouraged Max to reflect on why responsibility mattered, not just in finding lost things but in caring for them in the first place.

"Responsibility isn't just about fixing something after it goes wrong," Sol explained gently, his feathers ruffling in the breeze. "It's about being careful from the start. Think of it as a way of showing respect for the things we have and the promises we make."

Max listened closely, realizing how much he wanted to honor the promise he'd made to his mom about taking care of his new mittens. He felt a pang of regret for not being more careful that first day, but Sol's presence was calming. Max knew that, even if he hadn't been as responsible then, he could start now by giving his best effort to make things right.

As they searched the area near the slide, Max focused on each detail, carefully checking every nook and cranny around the equipment. Sol watched him patiently, offering words of encouragement.

"You're doing very well, Max," Sol said, his voice warm with approval. "Taking responsibility also means accepting when things don't go as planned and learning from those moments. Each step you take now is helping you grow."

Max felt a sense of pride as he continued his search. Though he hadn't found his mittens yet, he felt like he was learning a lesson he'd carry with him, even beyond this search. He started to realize that being responsible meant caring for things because they mattered, not just because they were useful.

After searching near the slide, they moved to the fence where Max had sometimes leaned while watching his friends play. Sol suggested they carefully check along the edge of the fence, where items could easily slip out of sight.

As they searched, Sol told Max about a time when he had lost a small, precious feather of his own. "One day, I lost a feather that was very special to me, and I searched everywhere. I learned that taking responsibility for our things doesn't mean we'll never lose them—it just means that when we do, we'll handle the situation with care."

Max nodded, touched by Sol's story. "It's like you learned from losing your feather the same way I'm learning from losing my mittens. Even if I don't find them, I'll always remember this experience."

Sol smiled, pleased with Max's growing understanding. "Exactly, Max. When we take responsibility, it helps us grow stronger and wiser. It's not just about finding the mittens; it's about how we approach the journey and the lessons we carry forward."

Their final stop was near the bushes at the edge of the playground, where Max had thrown his last snowball before going inside. He searched carefully around the bushes, moving each branch aside and checking beneath the snow. Though he still didn't find his mittens, he felt a sense of satisfaction knowing he had truly tried his best.

Chapter 9: Honesty with Mr. Ponder the Tortoise

The next morning, as Max arrived at school, he felt a familiar pang of worry. Despite his best efforts, his mittens were still missing. Though he had learned patience, teamwork, responsibility, and many valuable skills, he hadn't yet found them. Max knew it was time to be honest with someone he had been avoiding—his teacher, Mr. Ponder, a wise, thoughtful tortoise who always encouraged his students to be open and truthful, no matter how hard it seemed.

Max had been dreading this conversation, as he knew Mr. Ponder cared a lot about each student's well-being. Max worried that he might disappoint his teacher by admitting he'd lost something his mom had bought him so carefully. But deep down, he knew that talking to Mr. Ponder was the right thing to do. He took a deep breath and waited until recess, then approached his teacher's desk, feeling his heart thump nervously.

"Mr. Ponder?" Max said softly, shuffling his feet. "Can I talk to you about something?"

Mr. Ponder looked up with a warm, gentle smile. "Of course, Max. I'm always here to listen. What's on your mind?"

Max hesitated, gathering his courage. "I... I lost my new mittens, Mr. Ponder. I promised my mom I'd be careful with them, but I got distracted, and they just disappeared. I've been looking for them every day, but I haven't told her yet. I feel really bad about it."

Mr. Ponder nodded, his eyes kind and understanding. "Thank you for sharing that with me, Max. It takes courage to be honest, especially when we're afraid of disappointing someone. But honesty is a powerful tool, one that can help us grow and feel lighter. Have you considered telling your mom the truth?"

Max swallowed, feeling his cheeks warm. "I thought about it, but I was scared she'd be upset with me. She got me those mittens because I needed them, and I feel like I let her down."

Mr. Ponder placed a reassuring paw on Max's shoulder. "Being honest isn't always easy, Max, but it's often the best choice. When we tell the truth, we show respect to those we care about and give them a chance to understand us better. Hiding the truth only creates a barrier between us and the people who care for us."

Max listened intently, feeling a sense of relief wash over him as Mr. Ponder's words sank in. He realized that being honest might not be as scary as he'd thought; instead, it could bring him closer to his mom and help her understand what he'd been going through.

With Mr. Ponder's gentle encouragement, Max decided to practice honesty right away by explaining exactly how he lost his mittens. He told Mr. Ponder about each place he had checked and the friends who had helped him search.

Mr. Ponder listened patiently, nodding as Max spoke. When he was finished, Mr. Ponder said, "You've done a wonderful job in your search, Max, and you've learned so much along the way. Mistakes happen to everyone, and what truly matters is how we respond to them. Honesty helps us face those mistakes, learn from them, and move forward."

Max felt his spirits lift. "Thank you, Mr. Ponder. I think I'm ready to tell my mom the truth. I don't want her to worry or think I'm hiding things from her."

Mr. Ponder's face lit up with approval. "That's the spirit, Max! Honesty not only makes us stronger, but it also brings us closer to those who love us. And you know, your mom might be more understanding than you think."

After school, Max made up his mind. He would tell his mom the whole story. He had been holding onto his worry for so long that the idea of finally sharing it felt like a relief.

When he got home, he found his mom in the kitchen, preparing dinner. She looked up with a smile as he entered. "Hi, Max! How was school today?"

Max took a deep breath, his heart pounding. "Mom, can I talk to you about something important?"

She put down her spoon and turned to face him, her eyes full of gentle curiosity. "Of course, honey. What's on your mind?"

Max took a shaky breath, gathering his courage. "I... I lost my new mittens. I didn't mean to, but I was playing tag with Tully, and they must have slipped off. I've been looking for them every day with my friends, and I tried my best to find them, but they're still missing. I should have told you sooner, but I was scared you'd be disappointed."

His mom looked at him for a long moment, and Max braced himself for her reaction. But to his surprise, she didn't look angry. Instead, her face softened, and she reached out to pull him into a warm hug.

"Oh, Max," she said gently, stroking his hair. "Thank you for telling me. I'm not disappointed in you. I know how much you loved those mittens, and I can see you've been trying your best. It takes a lot of courage to be honest, and I'm so proud of you for telling me."

Max felt a wave of relief wash over him as he hugged her back. All the worry he'd been carrying seemed to melt away, replaced by a comforting sense of trust. He realized now that honesty had been the right choice, and it had brought him even closer to his mom.

After their talk, his mom suggested they check his usual spots together, retracing his steps with fresh eyes. "Sometimes, two sets of eyes are better than one," she said with a smile.

They went out into the yard, and Max led his mom along the path he usually took to school, sharing all the details of his search so far. As they walked, he felt a renewed sense of hope. Telling his mom the truth had lifted a weight from his shoulders, and now he felt more determined than ever to keep trying.

As they reached the park where he had played with Tully, his mom gave him a reassuring pat on the back. "Max, you've learned so much through this search, and that's more important than any pair of mittens. But I have a feeling they're out there, waiting for you to find them."

Max nodded, feeling his mom's support strengthen his resolve. Together, they checked under the bushes, along the benches, and near the trees where he had played. They didn't find the mittens, but Max didn't feel disappointed. He knew now that he was supported, no matter what, and that honesty had brought him closer to both his mom and Mr. Ponder.

Later that evening, Max reflected on all he had learned from his journey so far. Each friend had taught him something valuable, but today's lesson felt different. Honesty, he realized, wasn't just about telling the truth to avoid trouble; it was a way of building trust and showing respect for those he cared about.

He thought about Mr. Ponder's words, and how his mom's reaction had made him feel safe and understood. Being honest had turned out to be one of the most important steps he'd taken, and he was grateful for the courage he'd found to face his mistake.

Chapter 10: Positivity with Piper the Duckling

The next day, Max arrived at school with a lighter heart. Talking to his mom and Mr. Ponder about his missing mittens had helped him feel more at ease. His honesty had brought him comfort, and he felt closer to his family and teachers as a result. But he was still determined to find his mittens, and he knew he would need to approach the search with a fresh outlook. Today, Max decided to focus on staying positive, no matter what happened.

As he scanned the playground, Max spotted his cheerful friend Piper, a bubbly duckling with a bright yellow beak and a boundless love for adventure. Piper was always laughing, always finding the good in every situation, no matter how tough it seemed. Max knew that Piper's positivity could be just what he needed to bring a new spirit to his search.

"Hey, Piper!" Max called, waving as he approached her. "I was wondering if you'd like to help me look for my mittens today."

Piper's eyes sparkled with excitement. "Absolutely, Max! I'd love to help. And don't worry—we'll have a great time, no matter what! Who knows? Maybe today's the day we find them!"

Max felt his heart lift at her enthusiasm. Piper's optimistic energy was contagious, and he couldn't help but smile back. "Thanks, Piper. I think I really need some of your positive thinking. I've been searching for days now, and even though I haven't found them yet, I feel hopeful today."

Piper nodded, her beak curving into a wide smile. "That's the spirit, Max! Positivity is like a little light inside us. Even when things seem hard, it helps us see the good and keep going. Now, let's start searching!"

They began their search at the sandbox, a popular spot for the younger kids to play. Piper pranced around the sandbox, her small feet kicking up little puffs of snow as she inspected every corner with gleeful enthusiasm.

Max watched her, feeling a sense of joy as Piper approached the search like a fun game. "You really have a way of making everything feel exciting, Piper," he said, grinning.

Piper laughed, her voice ringing out like a tiny bell. "That's because I believe every moment is special, Max! And I know that, even if we don't find your mittens right away, we're going to have a lot of fun trying. Sometimes, the journey itself is the best part."

Max took her words to heart as they combed through the sandbox, using small sticks to gently poke through the snow in case his mittens were buried beneath the surface. Although they didn't find anything yet, Max found himself laughing along with Piper as she told funny stories about her other adventures.

After the sandbox, Piper suggested they check near the big tree at the edge of the playground. "Big trees are like nature's hiding spots," she said, her eyes twinkling. "Maybe your mittens are waiting there, just out of sight!"

They made their way to the tree, and Max began checking around the roots while Piper searched higher up, her beak curiously nudging the branches. They laughed as a gust of wind shook the tree, dusting them with snowflakes. Instead of feeling frustrated at the empty search, Max found himself enjoying the moment, feeling grateful for Piper's uplifting spirit.

As they continued their search, Max asked, "Piper, how do you always stay so positive? Even when things don't go the way you want?"

Piper smiled and paused for a moment, her wings folded gently at her sides. "I think about all the wonderful things that could still happen, Max. Sometimes, it's not about finding what we're looking for right away; it's about keeping our hearts open to all the good things along the way."

Her words touched Max, and he realized that keeping a positive outlook made every step of the journey feel lighter. Though he hadn't found his mittens, he could appreciate the joy of searching with a friend who made each moment feel special.

Their next stop was the snowy path that led toward the school's back gate. As they walked, Piper hummed a cheerful tune, occasionally stopping to point out interesting things along the way: a little trail of bird footprints, a bright red berry peeking out from the snow, and even a tiny icicle hanging from a branch.

"See, Max?" she said, pointing to the berry. "There's beauty all around us, even when we're looking for something else. If we only focus on what we don't have, we miss out on all the wonderful things we do have."

Max nodded, feeling a sense of warmth in his heart. "You're right, Piper. I've been so focused on finding my mittens that I almost forgot to appreciate everything else."

With Piper's guidance, Max began to notice the little details that made their search special. The way the snow sparkled in the sunlight, the cheerful chirping of nearby birds, and the gentle crunch of the snow beneath their feet. Each moment felt brighter, and Max felt grateful for the beauty around him.

Chapter 11: Helping Others with Mrs. Mallow and the Marketplace

On the eleventh day of his search, Max decided to take his efforts beyond the playground and school. He had covered most of the familiar areas around the schoolyard with the help of his friends, so he thought it might be time to explore a new place. After school, Max made his way to the marketplace in town, a lively spot filled with small shops, colorful stalls, and friendly neighbors who sold everything from fresh vegetables to cozy scarves.

Max's mom often took him to the marketplace on weekends, and he knew many of the vendors well. Today, he hoped that someone might have seen his mittens or perhaps even picked them up. But as he arrived, he saw Mrs. Mallow, a kind and elderly hare who sold baked goods, struggling to carry a large box of fresh loaves into her stall.

Without hesitation, Max hurried over, setting his own search aside for a moment. "Here, Mrs. Mallow, let me help you with that!"

Mrs. Mallow looked up in surprise, her whiskers twitching with gratitude. "Oh, thank you, Max! You're so thoughtful. I've been baking since early morning, and these old paws aren't as strong as they used to be."

Max carefully took the box and carried it into her stall, setting it down gently on the wooden counter. Mrs. Mallow beamed at him, patting his shoulder with a soft, wrinkled paw. "Thank you, dear. It's always nice to see young ones willing to lend a helping hand. Now, what brings you to the marketplace this afternoon?"

Max hesitated, then decided to share his story. "Well, Mrs. Mallow, I lost my mittens last week, and I've been searching for them every day. I thought maybe someone here might have found them."

Mrs. Mallow listened attentively, her face filled with sympathy. "Oh, dear, I can imagine how much that must be weighing on you.

Mittens are important, especially in this chilly weather! Tell you what—how about I keep an eye out, and if I see or hear anything about a pair of blue mittens with little white snowflakes, I'll let you know?"

Max's face lit up. "Thank you, Mrs. Mallow! That would mean so much."

As Max turned to continue his search, Mrs. Mallow called him back. "Hold on just a moment, Max! How would you like a cookie for the road? Consider it a thank-you for your help with my box."

Max smiled and gratefully accepted the warm, soft cookie she handed him. The gesture made him feel appreciated, and he realized that helping others brought its own kind of warmth, one that lifted his spirits and gave him strength.

With his cookie in hand, Max moved through the bustling marketplace, asking vendors if they had seen his mittens. He approached Mr. Finch, the owner of a small produce stall, and explained his situation.

"Good afternoon, Mr. Finch! I'm looking for my blue mittens. I lost them last week, and I thought maybe someone might have picked them up and brought them here?"

Mr. Finch, a cheerful squirrel with a red-and-white apron, scratched his chin thoughtfully. "Blue mittens with snowflakes, you say? I haven't seen any mittens myself, but I'll spread the word. There's always someone who knows someone in a place like this."

Max thanked him and continued on, stopping at each stall to ask the same question. Though he didn't find any clues, he noticed how willing everyone was to help. Vendors who barely knew him promised to keep an eye out, and many even offered him encouraging smiles and pats on the shoulder. The kindness he encountered warmed him from the inside out, and Max felt a renewed sense of gratitude for the community around him.

As he walked through the marketplace, he spotted a little sparrow struggling to carry a large berry in her beak. The berry was almost as big as her head, and she seemed determined, but clearly having trouble.

Max crouched down and extended a gentle hand. "Would you like some help with that?"

The sparrow looked at him gratefully, dropping the berry into his palm with a tired chirp. Max gently placed the berry in a small nook near the sparrow's perch, and she chirped her thanks before flying up to enjoy her treat. Helping her took only a moment, but it left Max feeling lighter and more connected to the world around him.

As the sun began to dip in the sky, Max decided to check in with a few more stalls before heading home. He stopped by the scarf stand, where Mrs. Cleary, a cheerful, chubby raccoon, was selling hand-knitted scarves of every color.

"Hello, Mrs. Cleary," Max said, smiling as he admired the scarves. "Have you seen any blue mittens with white snowflakes by any chance?"

Mrs. Cleary's eyes lit up with recognition. "Oh, Max, I haven't, but those sound lovely! I'll keep a lookout for you, and if I spot anything, you'll be the first to know."

Max thanked her, feeling another small spark of hope. He realized that asking for help wasn't only about finding his mittens—it was also about connecting with others, sharing his story, and allowing people to care for him. With each conversation, he felt less alone in his search.

As Max made his way toward the marketplace exit, he noticed a young rabbit trying to tie his shoelaces. The rabbit looked frustrated, his ears drooping as he struggled to make the laces stay in place. Without hesitation, Max walked over and knelt beside him.

"Need a little help with those laces?" he asked kindly.

The young rabbit nodded, looking relieved. Max showed him how to loop the laces around, forming a neat, sturdy bow. "There you go! It just takes a little practice."

The rabbit grinned, his face lighting up. "Thanks, Max! I always have trouble with my laces."

Max smiled back, feeling a warm sense of satisfaction. Helping others, he realized, didn't just make him feel good—it gave him a sense of purpose beyond his own worries. Though he hadn't found his mittens yet, he felt that his journey was becoming more meaningful through the small acts of kindness he shared along the way.

Chapter 12: Carefulness with Ollie the Otter

Max's search continued into the twelfth day, each lesson he learned from his friends shaping his journey in new ways. By now, he had realized that his search for his missing mittens was about more than just finding a pair of gloves—it was teaching him important values that he could carry with him forever. Today, he decided to focus on a skill he knew he would need if he wanted to become more responsible: carefulness.

After school, Max spotted his friend Ollie, a calm and thoughtful otter who was known for being exceptionally precise in everything he did. Ollie was always careful, whether he was building something, solving a problem, or playing with friends. Max knew that Ollie's meticulous approach could be exactly what he needed to bring a new perspective to his search.

"Hey, Ollie!" Max called, jogging over to his friend. "I could use some help with my mitten search. I've looked everywhere, but I think I might need to be more careful in how I look."

Ollie looked up with a friendly smile, his sleek fur shining in the afternoon light. "Sure thing, Max! I'd be happy to help. Carefulness is all about paying close attention, even to the smallest details, and being mindful of each step. It's easy to miss something if we're rushing, so let's take our time."

Max felt encouraged by Ollie's calm demeanor and nodded enthusiastically. "That sounds perfect, Ollie. Let's start with the playground, since that's where I last remember having my mittens."

The two friends made their way to the playground, and Ollie suggested they begin near the big oak tree where Max and Tully had played earlier in the week. But this time, Ollie showed Max how to slow down and look carefully at every detail.

"Instead of scanning the area quickly, try examining each spot closely," Ollie explained. "Sometimes, when we're in a hurry, we overlook things that are right in front of us."

Max nodded, crouching down next to Ollie as they began their search. Together, they gently moved aside leaves, checked beneath branches, and examined each patch of snow with careful eyes. Max found that by slowing down, he could see things he hadn't noticed before—a tiny acorn, a piece of colorful string, and even a small, shiny pebble. Though none of these were his mittens, Max began to appreciate the art of careful observation.

Ollie, sensing Max's focus, smiled and encouraged him. "You're doing great, Max. Carefulness isn't just about looking—it's about thinking, too. Each time you search, ask yourself if there's a spot you might have missed or if there's a new way to look at something."

Max took Ollie's advice to heart, feeling his patience grow as he continued their search. Together, they moved to the base of the slide, where Max remembered playing tag. Instead of just glancing around, they checked each corner of the slide, even lifting the edges of the soft snow to see if anything was hidden beneath.

After finishing their search around the playground, Ollie suggested they head toward the school's bike racks. "I know it might seem unlikely, but sometimes being thorough means checking even the places we don't expect," Ollie said thoughtfully. "Carefulness means covering all your bases, so let's make sure we don't miss anything."

At the bike racks, they inspected each area, moving slowly and methodically. Max noticed how Ollie examined every part of the ground, even the smallest cracks in the pavement, as though he expected each one to hold a secret. Max found himself mirroring Ollie's careful approach, and he began to feel a sense of satisfaction in knowing he was leaving no stone unturned.

Max smiled at Ollie, feeling a sense of pride in their shared effort. "I feel like I'm really learning something here, Ollie. Taking my time and being careful is actually kind of relaxing. It's like I can appreciate the little things I might have missed."

Ollie nodded approvingly. "Exactly, Max! Carefulness doesn't just help us find things; it also helps us understand the world better. When we're careful, we see details and patterns we might have missed, and we can avoid making mistakes that we'd regret later."

Max thought about how he'd lost his mittens in the first place. He realized that he hadn't been careful then; he'd been caught up in the excitement of playing, and the mittens had slipped away without him noticing. Now, though, he felt he was learning to be more mindful, both in searching and in how he cared for his things.

Their next stop was near the bushes by the school's fence. Max recalled how he'd leaned against the fence while playing tag with Tully, and he wanted to make sure he hadn't missed anything there.

This time, Ollie showed him how to examine each branch, gently moving them aside one by one. Max was impressed by Ollie's patience, and he tried to follow his example, carefully inspecting every part of the bush. Though he didn't find his mittens, he felt a growing sense of pride in his ability to search with patience and precision.

As they continued their search, Ollie shared a story that helped Max understand the importance of carefulness. "Once, I built a little raft to use on the pond near my home," Ollie began, his voice soft and thoughtful. "I was so eager to test it that I skipped some steps, thinking it would be fine. But when I put the raft on the water, it started to sink because I hadn't carefully checked the knots and boards."

Max listened, captivated by Ollie's story. "Oh no! What did you do?"

Ollie chuckled. "I learned a valuable lesson that day. After that, I started taking my time with each project, checking every detail twice to make sure everything was secure. Since then, I haven't had any rafts sink on me!"

Max laughed, feeling inspired by Ollie's example. He realized that carefulness wasn't just about finding lost items—it was a way of approaching life with thoughtfulness and respect. Each time he searched, he was learning to care more deeply for the things around him, from the tiny acorns on the ground to the branches in the bushes.

As the afternoon wore on, Max and Ollie completed their search around the fence and moved to the far side of the playground. By now, Max felt a new sense of pride in his careful approach. Although they still hadn't found the mittens, Max knew he had left no area unchecked, and that brought him a sense of peace.

Before they finished, Ollie offered one final piece of advice. "Max, carefulness isn't just for searching. It's something you can practice every day, in everything you do. When you put care into your actions, it shows in the quality of your work and the way you treat others."

Chapter 13: Encouragement with Coach Bruno the Bear

By the thirteenth day of his search, Max's journey had taken him through so many different places and emotions. He had learned about patience, honesty, positivity, carefulness, and so much more from each friend who had helped him along the way. Yet, despite his best efforts, Max's mittens were still nowhere to be found.

Though he'd grown in so many ways, Max was starting to feel a bit discouraged. He wondered if he would ever see his mittens again. But as he made his way across the school field, he saw Coach Bruno, the strong but gentle bear who taught gym class. Coach Bruno was known for his supportive spirit, always ready to cheer his students on no matter what they were facing. Seeing him now, Max knew this was exactly the encouragement he needed.

"Coach Bruno!" Max called, jogging over. "Do you have a moment to talk?"

Coach Bruno turned, his eyes bright and warm. "Max! Of course, I always have time for one of my star students. What's on your mind?"

Max hesitated, feeling a bit embarrassed. "I've been looking for my mittens for almost two weeks now. I've had so much help, and I've learned a lot, but I'm starting to feel like I might never find them. I think... I think I'm losing hope."

Coach Bruno crouched down to Max's level, giving him an understanding nod. "I know it's hard to keep going when things don't go the way we hope, Max. But sometimes, a little encouragement is all we need to keep pushing forward. You've been so determined this whole time—don't give up now! Maybe all you need is a new approach."

Max looked up, feeling his spirits lift. "You really think so? I just don't want to keep looking if there's no chance I'll find them."

Coach Bruno placed a big, gentle paw on Max's shoulder. "I do think so, Max. Remember, it's not just about finding your mittens; it's about seeing how strong and resilient you can be. Let's make today a fresh start, and I'll help you with whatever you need."

Max smiled, his heart filling with a renewed sense of determination. "Thanks, Coach Bruno. I think I just needed a reminder that I can keep going."

Together, Max and Coach Bruno decided to start their search at the school's track. Coach Bruno suggested they jog around the track first to warm up. "Exercise can help clear your mind and make you feel more energized. Let's do a lap or two before we begin our search."

Max nodded, following Coach Bruno's lead as they began a light jog. As they ran, Max felt his spirits lift even more. The steady rhythm of his feet on the track helped him shake off his frustration, replacing it with a sense of focus and calm. By the time they finished their warm-up, Max felt ready to tackle the search with fresh energy.

"See? A little movement goes a long way," Coach Bruno said, patting Max on the back. "Now, let's get searching!"

They decided to start by checking the bleachers. Coach Bruno led Max to the rows of seats, showing him how to carefully look under each bench and along the sides where items might have rolled out of sight. Coach Bruno moved slowly, encouraging Max to check every corner as they went.

Max remembered what he'd learned from Ollie about being careful, and he applied it now, making sure not to rush. Coach Bruno's encouragement helped him stay positive, even when he didn't find anything right away. With each bench he checked, Max felt a little more hopeful, knowing he wasn't alone in his efforts.

After they finished searching the bleachers, Coach Bruno suggested they check the equipment shed. "It's where we keep all the sports gear, and sometimes students leave things in there by accident. Let's take a look!"

The shed was a small wooden structure filled with balls, jump ropes, and various sports supplies. Max had played near the shed during recess, so he thought it was possible his mittens could have ended up here. Coach Bruno opened the door, and together they began sorting through the equipment.

"Sometimes, when things don't show up where we expect, it just means we need to look at the problem from a different angle," Coach Bruno said, lifting a basket of jump ropes and checking underneath. "Think of this as a challenge. Challenges make us stronger, Max, and each one teaches us something new about ourselves."

Max nodded, encouraged by Coach Bruno's words. He carefully looked through the shelves, checking each corner and behind the equipment boxes. Though he didn't find his mittens, he felt his hope growing again, fueled by Coach Bruno's positive energy.

After they finished with the equipment shed, Coach Bruno suggested they search near the football field. "Sometimes, when we least expect it, things turn up where we hadn't thought to look before. Let's give the field a try!"

As they reached the field, Max noticed how Coach Bruno kept him motivated by setting small goals. "Let's check one corner at a time," he said. "Each area we cover is a small victory, even if we don't find anything. It's all about progress."

Max followed Coach Bruno's lead, feeling more optimistic with each section they searched. By focusing on small goals, the task didn't seem as overwhelming, and he found himself enjoying the process more than he had before. Coach Bruno's encouragement made each step feel meaningful, showing Max that even small achievements were worth celebrating.

They worked their way around the field, scanning the grass and the goalposts, even checking near the benches along the sidelines. Though they still hadn't found his mittens, Coach Bruno remained upbeat, giving Max a thumbs-up each time they completed a section.

Chapter 14: Listening and Wisdom with Grandma Hazel

After days of searching, Max felt he had tried almost everything to find his mittens. Each day brought new lessons from friends and mentors who encouraged him, helped him grow, and lifted his spirits. Yet, despite his best efforts, his mittens remained lost. He felt he was running out of ideas on where to look or what to try next. That's when Max decided it was time to visit someone very special—his Grandma Hazel.

Grandma Hazel was known for her wisdom and calm presence. She was the person everyone in the family turned to for advice, and Max had always loved listening to her stories and learning from her gentle, thoughtful words. Today, he hoped that Grandma Hazel could offer some fresh insight into his mitten mystery.

After school, Max made his way to his grandmother's cozy cottage on the edge of town. The path to her home was lined with tall trees and winding bushes, and Max felt a sense of peace as he walked, listening to the crunch of leaves beneath his feet. When he reached the front door, he knocked softly, feeling a wave of comfort wash over him.

"Come in, dear!" Grandma Hazel's warm voice called from inside.

Max opened the door and found her sitting in her favorite chair by the fireplace, knitting a soft, blue scarf. She looked up and smiled, her eyes twinkling with kindness. "Max, what a lovely surprise! What brings you here today?"

Max hesitated, but her warm smile put him at ease. He sat down next to her, feeling the warmth of the fire on his cheeks. "Grandma, I lost my mittens a while ago. I've searched everywhere, and my friends have all helped me, but I still can't find them. I thought maybe you could help me figure out what to do next."

Grandma Hazel set down her knitting, her gaze thoughtful as she looked at Max. "Oh, my dear, that sounds like quite a journey you've been on. I can tell you've tried hard, and sometimes, when we've done all we can, it helps to stop and listen, to let our hearts guide us."

Max tilted his head, listening closely. "You mean... listen to my heart? I haven't tried that before."

Grandma Hazel nodded, her eyes wise and knowing. "Yes, Max. Listening is a skill that takes practice, just like searching or being careful. It's about paying attention, not just to the world around you but also to what's inside of you. Sometimes, our hearts have answers that our minds can't see."

Max thought about her words, feeling curious. He closed his eyes for a moment, trying to focus on what his heart might be telling him. But instead of a clear answer, he felt a rush of memories—each friend who had helped him, every place he had searched, and all the lessons he had learned. He remembered the patience Tully had taught him, the carefulness from Ollie, and the encouragement from Coach Bruno.

When he opened his eyes, he looked at his grandmother. "I think my heart is telling me to keep going, even though it's hard. But it's also telling me to take a different approach, to try something I haven't thought of before."

Grandma Hazel smiled, patting his hand. "That's a wonderful insight, Max. Sometimes, listening helps us find the courage to try again. You've learned so much already, and I'm very proud of you. But here's something else to remember: wisdom often comes from reflection. Let's look back on your journey together and see if we can uncover any clues you may have missed."

Max agreed, feeling a spark of hope. Grandma Hazel handed him a warm mug of tea and encouraged him to walk through each step of his search. Together, they began to retrace his journey, one memory at a time.

As they talked, Max remembered each detail with Grandma Hazel's gentle guidance. He shared how he had started his search in the playground with Tully, learning patience and focus. He recalled the fun he'd had with Piper, whose positivity lifted his spirits, and how Quinny had shown him the importance of teamwork. With each story, Grandma Hazel listened intently, her quiet presence helping Max see the value of every lesson.

When they reached the part about being honest with his mom and Mr. Ponder, Grandma Hazel's smile grew even warmer. "Honesty is a powerful virtue, Max. It opens doors to understanding and shows others that we're willing to grow. You've done so well, learning each lesson along the way."

Max nodded, feeling the warmth of her words. But as he recounted his story, he realized he had been so focused on each individual lesson that he hadn't looked at the journey as a whole.

"That's it, Grandma! I think I understand now," Max said excitedly. "I've been searching piece by piece, place by place, but maybe I need to look at everything together. Like a puzzle that needs all the pieces to be complete."

Grandma Hazel chuckled, giving him a proud nod. "Exactly, my dear. Wisdom comes not just from what we learn, but from how we bring all those lessons together. Your journey isn't just about finding your mittens; it's about understanding what you've gained along the way."

With Grandma Hazel's advice fresh in his mind, Max decided to make one last effort, but this time with a new perspective. Instead of just searching one place at a time, he would reflect on everything he had learned and apply each lesson at once. His grandmother's words had given him a new sense of hope, and he felt more ready than ever to continue.

Before he left, Grandma Hazel hugged him tightly. "Remember, Max, wisdom often comes in quiet moments. If you're ever unsure, take a moment to listen. You'll find that your heart often knows the way."

Max hugged her back, feeling a deep sense of gratitude. "Thank you, Grandma. I'll remember to listen, and I'll try to use all the lessons my friends taught me."

As he walked back home, Max felt like he had a new sense of purpose. His grandmother's wisdom was like a gentle light, guiding him forward. He wasn't just looking for his mittens anymore; he was looking to bring all his newfound understanding into every step he took.

The next day, Max returned to school with a clear mind and a calm heart. He decided to start by applying Ollie's carefulness and Whisk's attention to detail, searching in areas he hadn't fully explored. This time, he combined his carefulness with Tully's patience, not rushing but instead savoring each small moment as he retraced his steps.

As he searched, he remembered Piper's positivity and tried to keep his spirits high, even when he didn't find anything right away. Each time he thought of giving up, he recalled Coach Bruno's encouragement and set small goals, celebrating each small section he checked.

After school, he stopped by the park where he had first played tag with Tully, carefully checking around the trees and bushes with all the skills he'd learned. With each step, he felt Grandma Hazel's wisdom guiding him, reminding him to listen, reflect, and find meaning in every part of the journey.

Finally, just as he was about to finish his search for the day, something caught his eye near the edge of the bushes—a small blue shape, half-buried in the snow. Max's heart leaped as he carefully approached, his excitement bubbling over as he reached down and pulled out a mitten, his mitten! And just a few steps away, nestled against the base of a tree, was the second mitten.

Max's eyes filled with happy tears as he held his mittens close, feeling a rush of joy and gratitude. His friends' support, his family's love, and his grandmother's wisdom had all led him here, bringing him back to what he had been searching for all along.

That evening, Max visited Grandma Hazel to share the good news. She listened with a warm smile as he told her everything, from finding the mitten to how he had used each lesson to guide him.

Chapter 15: Problem-Solving with Finn the Squirrel

The next day, after finding his mittens with the guidance of his friends and Grandma Hazel's wisdom, Max felt a deep sense of gratitude. He realized that his journey wasn't just about solving a problem but about learning valuable life lessons from each friend. Max was excited to return to school and share his story with everyone, but he also had a special purpose for the day. There was one more friend who had offered to help him in a unique way: Finn, the creative and clever squirrel.

Finn was known for his incredible problem-solving skills. He could turn any puzzle or challenge into a fun project, finding solutions where others saw dead-ends. Finn had even built his own tiny pulley system out of branches and vines, helping him retrieve acorns from high tree branches. Max admired Finn's creativity and looked forward to learning from him, knowing that problem-solving was a skill he could always use.

"Hey, Finn!" Max called when he spotted the squirrel near the playground. "I found my mittens! But I still want to learn about problem-solving from you. I think it could help me with other challenges."

Finn's eyes sparkled with excitement as he scampered over. "That's fantastic, Max! I'd be thrilled to share some problem-solving tricks with you. You know, problem-solving isn't just about fixing what's wrong; it's also about finding new ways to look at things. Let's do some exercises to build your skills!"

Max grinned, eager to start. He could already feel the excitement of learning something new with Finn, whose enthusiasm made even the hardest challenges feel like games.

Finn led Max to a small table under the oak tree near the school, where he had set up a few small puzzles and objects he'd collected.

"Problem-solving is like a treasure hunt," Finn explained, pointing to a simple puzzle made of sticks and twine. "First, you look at the pieces you have, then you imagine how they can come together."

Max picked up the puzzle, studying it carefully. Finn guided him to consider each piece, not just as it was but as part of a larger picture. "Sometimes, you have to look beyond what's in front of you," Finn said. "Imagine each part in different ways. What could you use to connect these pieces? What might make the puzzle come together?"

Max turned the pieces over in his hands, taking time to think. He tried placing them together in different ways, discovering that he could rearrange them to form a small bridge if he tied them carefully with the twine. With Finn's guidance, he finally figured out the puzzle, smiling with satisfaction.

"Great job, Max!" Finn cheered. "That's the first step of problem-solving—exploring possibilities. Never be afraid to try something new, even if it doesn't work the first time."

Max nodded, feeling a sense of accomplishment. "I get it! It's like when I was looking for my mittens. Each new place I searched was like trying a new piece of the puzzle."

Next, Finn decided to introduce Max to another aspect of problem-solving: breaking down a big task into smaller steps. He took Max to the edge of the field, where a small pile of stones had been left from a landscaping project. The stones were too big to lift all at once, but Finn had a creative idea.

"Let's say your goal is to move all these stones from here to the sandbox," Finn said, pointing to the sandbox on the other side of the field. "It seems impossible if you try to do it all at once, right?"

Max looked at the stones and nodded, feeling a bit daunted by the task. "Yeah, that would be hard."

Finn grinned, tapping one of the smaller stones with his paw. "But if we break it down into smaller steps, it's totally doable. Watch this."

Finn began moving a few stones at a time, carrying the smaller ones and rolling the bigger ones a little bit at a time. Max quickly joined in, working with Finn to transport each stone in small, manageable steps. Before long, they had moved half of the pile, and Max could see the progress they were making.

"This is amazing, Finn! It's way easier than trying to move everything at once," Max said, feeling energized by their progress.

"That's the magic of problem-solving, Max," Finn said, smiling as he placed another stone in the sandbox. "When you break a big problem into smaller parts, it doesn't seem so overwhelming. And working together makes it even easier."

Max realized that breaking down tasks was something he could apply to other parts of his life, too. He thought about how he'd felt overwhelmed at the beginning of his mitten search, but dividing it into steps had helped him manage it one piece at a time.

After finishing with the stones, Finn introduced another skill: creative thinking. He brought Max over to a patch of dirt where he'd drawn different patterns with his paws. Some were circles, some were zigzags, and others formed spirals.

"Creative thinking is about seeing things differently," Finn explained. "Sometimes, solving a problem isn't about doing the same thing over and over—it's about finding a new way to look at it. Let's play a game. Try to connect these patterns with your finger, but don't lift it off the ground."

Max looked at the patterns, feeling puzzled at first. He tried a few ways, lifting his finger and starting again. After several tries, he realized he could solve it by combining two lines together, which allowed him to trace the pattern without lifting his finger.

Finn clapped his paws together, grinning. "Exactly, Max! You found a new way to look at the problem. Creative thinking helps you see different possibilities that aren't obvious at first. It's like when you found your mittens—you had to think about all the lessons from your friends to finally figure it out."

Max felt a sense of pride. Finn's exercises were not only fun but were teaching him new ways of seeing the world. "Thank you, Finn! This is really helping me understand how to tackle challenges."

Finn decided to finish the day by teaching Max about one final aspect of problem-solving: staying calm under pressure. He led Max to a spot near the pond, where they could see their reflections in the water. "Sometimes, when things go wrong, it's easy to feel frustrated or upset," Finn said. "But one of the best ways to solve a problem is to stay calm, even when things get tough."

Max shook his head, remembering moments during his search when he had felt overwhelmed or frustrated. "You're right, Finn. It was hard sometimes, and I felt like giving up. But I kept going because my friends helped me stay positive."

Finn encouraged Max to look at his reflection in the water. "Whenever you feel frustrated, take a deep breath and focus on what you can do. Staying calm helps clear your mind and makes it easier to think clearly. You've done this already, Max, even if you didn't realize it. That's a part of problem-solving, too!"

Chapter 16: Adaptability with Faye the Fox

Max's journey had been full of lessons from friends who had each helped him in their unique way. His problem-solving practice with Finn had given him the skills to approach challenges with creativity and a calm mind. But as he continued to think about all the lessons he had learned, he realized there was one skill he still needed: adaptability.

Adaptability, he remembered, meant being flexible and able to handle unexpected changes. Max knew this would be valuable, especially since his search for his mittens had been filled with surprises. To learn more about adaptability, he turned to his friend Faye, a quick and clever fox known for her ability to navigate any situation with ease.

Max found Faye near the wooded edge of the playground, where she was busy weaving her way through a little maze she had built from fallen branches. She moved gracefully, never hesitating, even as she twisted and turned through the narrow paths.

"Hey, Faye!" Max called, watching her with admiration. "I've learned so much from my friends, but I think I could use some help with learning to adapt. You're always so flexible and quick to handle things. Can you teach me?"

Faye's eyes sparkled with excitement as she hopped over a branch to meet him. "Of course, Max! Adaptability is all about being ready to adjust when things don't go as planned. Life is full of surprises, and being adaptable helps you go with the flow. Let's go through a few exercises to get you in the spirit!"

Max felt a thrill of anticipation. He had seen how Faye's adaptability made her a natural leader in challenging situations, and he looked forward to learning her techniques.

Faye started with a simple exercise. She led Max to the edge of the playground, where there were clusters of rocks and branches scattered about. "Alright, Max," Faye said, pointing to the rocks. "Imagine you're on a journey, but each time you step on a rock, you have to change direction. This will help you get used to making quick decisions."

Max stepped onto the first rock and paused, unsure of which way to go. Faye encouraged him to pick a direction without thinking too hard about it. "Remember, Max, adaptability is about moving forward even if the path changes. Just keep adjusting and trust yourself!"

Max took a deep breath and hopped onto another rock, quickly choosing his next move. Each time he stepped, he faced a different direction, learning to make quick decisions without overthinking. At first, it felt strange, but as he continued, he began to enjoy the process, finding new routes and adjusting with each step.

"Great job, Max!" Faye cheered as he completed the exercise. "See? You're already getting better at making adjustments on the go."

Max grinned, feeling a sense of accomplishment. "It's actually kind of fun! I didn't know making quick decisions could feel so natural."

Faye smiled, giving him a playful nudge. "Exactly! The more you practice, the easier it becomes. And remember, adapting isn't just about reacting; it's about feeling confident that you can handle whatever comes your way."

For the next exercise, Faye led Max to a trail near the playground that twisted and turned through tall grass. This time, Faye told Max to follow her lead, but with a twist: each time she stopped and changed direction, Max had to do the same.

They started slowly, with Faye moving at an easy pace. Each time she changed direction, she paused to give Max a moment to adjust. But soon, she began to speed up, making quick turns and leading him through unexpected paths. Max had to stay alert, his eyes focused on Faye as he matched her every move. Each twist and turn taught him to stay flexible, ready to change course at a moment's notice.

"Adaptability means staying alert and open to change, Max," Faye said as they weaved through the trail. "It's like a dance with the world around you. The better you get at adjusting, the more smoothly you move through life."

Max felt a rush of excitement as he kept pace with Faye. Though the path was unpredictable, he enjoyed the challenge, and he realized that adapting quickly was making him feel more confident. By the end of the exercise, Max felt as though he'd gained a new perspective, one that allowed him to embrace change rather than resist it.

After finishing the trail exercise, Faye introduced Max to another way of practicing adaptability: creating a plan while being prepared to let it go. She took him to the edge of the playground and pointed to a line of stones leading to a large tree.

"Let's create a path to that tree, but here's the challenge: each time you see something unexpected, you have to change your route," Faye explained. "It's a good way to practice having a flexible mindset, so you don't get too attached to a single way of doing things."

Max set off along the line of stones, focusing on the tree. He started carefully, placing his feet on each stone and planning his route. But halfway through, a branch blocked his way, forcing him to find a new path. At first, he felt frustrated by the interruption, but Faye's calm encouragement helped him stay focused.

"Remember, Max, adaptability is about embracing change, not fighting it. Look for new possibilities rather than dwelling on what didn't work."

Max nodded, stepping around the branch and finding a new path. Each time he encountered an obstacle, he adjusted, learning to see challenges as part of the journey. By the time he reached the tree, Max felt a sense of accomplishment. He had found a new way to approach challenges by remaining open to change.

For their final exercise, Faye and Max sat on a bench overlooking the playground. Faye shared her experience of adaptability in her own life, helping Max understand its importance on a deeper level.

Chapter 17: Resilience with Rocky the Badger

Max's journey of searching and learning had given him countless skills, yet he sensed there was still more to discover. Each friend had taught him something valuable, and he felt that these lessons had become part of who he was. However, there were still days when he felt a bit discouraged, especially when he remembered how long it had taken to find his mittens. Max realized that there was one more skill he wanted to master: resilience.

Resilience, he knew, was the ability to keep going even when things were hard, to bounce back from disappointment and not give up. He thought of Rocky, a strong and steadfast badger who was known for his determination. Rocky had a reputation for never giving up, even when faced with the most challenging tasks. Max knew that if anyone could teach him resilience, it was Rocky.

After school, Max found Rocky digging by the old garden bed near the playground. Rocky was always busy with a project, whether it was building burrows or collecting materials for his next adventure. Today, he was digging carefully around the roots of a small tree, his paws moving with steady determination.

"Hey, Rocky!" Max called out, watching as Rocky paused to wave him over. "I've been learning so much from my friends, and now that I've finally found my mittens, I feel like there's still one more thing I need to learn. Can you teach me about resilience?"

Rocky's eyes sparkled with interest, and he nodded with a grin. "Of course, Max! Resilience is about strength, but it's also about endurance. It's about keeping your heart strong, even when things get tough. Are you ready for a few resilience exercises?"

MAX'S MISSING MITTENS

Max nodded eagerly, feeling a sense of excitement. He was curious to learn how Rocky stayed so steady, no matter what challenges he faced.

Rocky started by introducing Max to the idea of persistence, which was a big part of resilience. He pointed to a large, heavy stone near the garden bed. "Let's say you need to move this stone from here to that corner over there. It's heavy, and it'll take time, but persistence means you don't give up, even if it takes many tries."

Max studied the stone, realizing it was too heavy to move in one go. He knew he'd have to try again and again, pushing a little each time. Rocky encouraged him, showing him how to find good handholds and use his legs to push rather than his arms.

"Think of each push as a step forward," Rocky said as Max began to push the stone. "You might only move it a little at a time, but each push brings you closer to your goal."

Max focused, pushing the stone with all his strength. It barely moved at first, but with each effort, he noticed it budging a bit more. Even when he felt tired, Rocky cheered him on, encouraging him to keep going. Eventually, after several tries, he moved the stone to the corner, feeling a rush of pride.

"You did it, Max!" Rocky clapped his paws together, smiling warmly. "That's what resilience looks like—small efforts that add up over time, helping you achieve big goals."

Max felt a surge of accomplishment. He realized that resilience wasn't just about being strong; it was about staying committed and pushing forward, no matter how slow the progress might seem.

For the next exercise, Rocky showed Max how to handle setbacks. He led Max to a small area where a tall grass hedge stood near a shallow ditch. Rocky explained that he would need to cross the ditch without stepping in it, which would require some trial and error.

"Sometimes, we'll face obstacles that we can't overcome right away," Rocky said, demonstrating by stepping over the ditch and nearly falling in. "But resilience means getting back up and trying again, even when we don't succeed the first time."

Max followed Rocky's lead, attempting to step over the ditch. His first try was wobbly, and he ended up slipping back, but Rocky encouraged him to try again. Each attempt taught Max a little more about balancing, where to place his feet, and how to keep his movements steady. With every failed attempt, he became more determined, and soon he was able to cross the ditch without slipping.

"See, Max?" Rocky said, grinning. "Each setback taught you something. Resilience means learning from each mistake and becoming stronger because of it."

Max nodded, feeling a sense of pride and understanding. He realized that resilience didn't mean avoiding failure; it meant finding the strength to keep going despite it.

Afterward, Rocky introduced Max to the idea of self-encouragement, a skill that could help him stay resilient even when he was on his own. He led Max to a small hill, suggesting that they climb it as a final exercise in resilience.

"It's easy to feel encouraged when others are cheering you on," Rocky explained, "but resilience is also about finding encouragement within yourself. Sometimes, when things get tough, you have to remind yourself that you're capable and that you can handle whatever comes your way."

Max took a deep breath, looking up at the hill. He began climbing, feeling his legs work as he made his way upward. Rocky climbed alongside him, but instead of offering encouragement, he remained quiet, letting Max find his own inner voice.

When Max began to feel tired halfway up, he took a moment to breathe, reminding himself that he had already overcome many challenges. He whispered to himself, "I can do this. I've learned so much, and I'm stronger because of it."

With renewed determination, Max continued climbing, step by step, until he finally reached the top. Rocky joined him, nodding with approval. "Great job, Max! You found strength within yourself, even when things got tough. That's resilience."

Max felt a swell of pride as he looked out over the view from the top of the hill. He realized that resilience wasn't just about pushing forward—it was about believing in himself and finding strength from within.

To end the day, Rocky shared a story that helped Max understand resilience on a deeper level. "There was a time," Rocky began, "when I was building a tunnel near my home. I ran into more rocks than I expected, and each one seemed to block my path. I got frustrated and almost gave up. But then I thought about why I was digging that tunnel—it was for my family, to create a safe place for us. Remembering that purpose gave me the strength to keep going."

Chapter 18: Gratitude with Louie the Owl

The journey of finding his mittens had changed Max in ways he hadn't expected. He had learned patience, honesty, teamwork, and resilience, and each lesson had helped him grow. But as he reflected on everything he had gained, he realized there was something more he wanted to explore—gratitude. Max had received so much help and support from his friends and family, and he wanted to learn how to fully appreciate it.

To learn more about gratitude, Max decided to visit Louie, a wise old owl who lived in a tree at the edge of the schoolyard. Louie was known for his deep understanding of life and was always encouraging others to be grateful for the little things. Max knew that Louie could help him understand how to feel and express gratitude in a meaningful way.

After school, Max made his way to Louie's tree. The evening sky was turning shades of pink and orange, casting a warm glow over the branches. Louie sat quietly, watching the sunset, his wise eyes reflecting the colors of the sky.

"Hello, Louie," Max said softly, not wanting to disturb the peaceful moment.

Louie turned his head slowly, a gentle smile appearing on his beak. "Ah, Max. What a pleasure to see you, my friend. Come, sit with me. What brings you here today?"

Max settled down next to the tree, looking up at Louie. "I've learned so much from my friends, and I'm really grateful for everything they've taught me. But sometimes I feel like I don't know how to show my gratitude. Can you help me understand it better?"

Louie nodded, his gaze thoughtful. "Gratitude, my dear Max, is like a seed. The more you nurture it, the more it grows, filling your heart with appreciation for the world around you. Gratitude is about recognizing the gifts we receive, no matter how small, and allowing them to bring us joy."

Max listened intently, feeling inspired by Louie's gentle wisdom. "How can I practice gratitude, Louie? I want to make sure my friends and family know how thankful I am."

Louie smiled, his eyes twinkling. "Let's explore some ways to show gratitude, Max. Sometimes, all it takes is a little reflection and a willingness to express our thanks."

To start, Louie encouraged Max to reflect on all the friends who had helped him find his mittens. He handed Max a small notebook and a pencil, suggesting he write down each friend's name and the lesson they had taught him.

"Writing it down helps you appreciate each person individually," Louie explained. "Take your time, and think about what each friend brought to your journey."

Max began to write, starting with Tully, who had taught him patience, and Rina, who had shown him the power of organization. He thought of Piper's positivity, Ollie's carefulness, and Finn's problem-solving skills. As he continued to write, he felt a deep sense of warmth and gratitude filling his heart.

When he finished, he looked up at Louie with a smile. "This really helped, Louie. Seeing everyone's names and lessons makes me realize how lucky I am to have such wonderful friends."

Louie nodded approvingly. "That's the magic of gratitude, Max. It reminds us of the blessings in our lives and helps us cherish the people who make our journey brighter."

Next, Louie suggested a small exercise to help Max express his gratitude. "Sometimes, the best way to show gratitude is to give back," Louie said, his voice soft and wise. "Think of something you can do for each friend to show them how much they mean to you. It doesn't have to be big—a simple gesture can speak volumes."

Max thought about each friend and what he could do to thank them. He decided he could give Tully a small snowball he had shaped perfectly, something he knew Tully would appreciate for their next game of tag. For Rina, he thought of making a small, organized list of fun things they could do together, just as she had shown him the power of organization. For Piper, he planned to bring a tiny feather he had found, knowing she loved little treasures.

As Max listed small, thoughtful gestures for each friend, he felt a growing sense of joy. Louie's advice was helping him see that gratitude wasn't just a feeling—it was something he could share with others.

After they finished the list, Louie shared another way to practice gratitude: by finding joy in everyday moments. He guided Max to close his eyes, take a deep breath, and simply listen to the sounds around them—the rustling leaves, the distant chirping of crickets, the soft breeze.

"Gratitude can be as simple as appreciating the beauty of this very moment," Louie said softly. "When we stop and notice the world around us, we realize how many small gifts fill our lives every day."

Max sat quietly, feeling the peacefulness of the moment. He noticed the coolness of the breeze, the warmth of the setting sun, and the steady comfort of Louie's presence beside him. In that moment, he felt connected to everything around him, realizing that gratitude didn't always need words. Sometimes, it was simply about being present and feeling the joy of being alive.

Chapter 19: Empathy with Mira the Deer

After days of learning and growing, Max had discovered countless values and virtues that had enriched his journey. His search for his mittens had evolved into a path of self-discovery, guided by the kindness and wisdom of each friend. One morning, as he thought about all the lessons he'd learned, Max realized there was one more virtue he wanted to understand better: empathy.

Empathy, he remembered from a story his teacher had shared, was the ability to feel what others were feeling and understand their experiences. Max felt that empathy was an important way to connect with others, but he wasn't sure how to practice it. He decided to visit Mira, a gentle deer who was known for her understanding heart and compassionate nature. Mira was often seen comforting others, and she had a way of making everyone around her feel heard and understood.

Max found Mira near the forest's edge, where she was gathering flowers to bring to her family. She looked up with a soft smile as Max approached, her eyes warm and inviting.

"Hello, Max," Mira greeted him gently. "What brings you to the forest today?"

Max took a deep breath, feeling grateful for Mira's kind welcome. "I've been learning a lot from my friends, but there's one more thing I want to understand better: empathy. I want to learn how to connect with others in a way that shows them I care. Can you help me?"

Mira's face softened, her gentle eyes reflecting kindness and understanding. "Of course, Max. Empathy is one of the most beautiful ways to show others that we care. It helps us understand each other's hearts and makes us feel connected. Let's go for a walk, and I'll show you a few ways to practice empathy."

Max smiled, feeling a sense of peace as he followed Mira into the forest. He knew that her wisdom would help him discover new ways to show kindness and compassion.

As they walked, Mira encouraged Max to listen closely to the sounds around them—the soft rustle of leaves, the birds chirping, and the gentle whisper of the wind through the trees.

"Empathy starts with listening, Max," Mira said, her voice soft and warm. "When we listen carefully, we can begin to understand the feelings of others, even when they don't say anything directly."

Max nodded, focusing on each sound. He realized that listening was about more than just hearing words—it was about paying attention, noticing small details, and truly being present. Mira's calm presence helped him feel connected to the world around him, and he began to appreciate the beauty of simply listening.

After a few minutes, they heard a faint rustling nearby. Mira led Max to a small clearing where a tiny rabbit was sitting alone, looking sad and lost. Mira paused, watching the rabbit with gentle concern.

"Let's try to understand how the rabbit might be feeling," Mira whispered. "Look closely at his body language and his expression. What do you think he might need?"

Max observed the rabbit carefully, noticing how it sat with its head lowered, its ears drooping. "I think he might be feeling lonely," Max said softly. "Maybe he needs someone to comfort him."

Mira nodded, her eyes warm with approval. "That's empathy, Max. You're noticing how he feels by observing his body language and trying to understand his emotions. Let's approach him gently and see if we can offer some comfort."

Together, they walked slowly toward the rabbit, keeping their movements gentle so as not to startle him. Mira spoke softly, offering soothing words, and Max crouched down, speaking in a kind voice. The rabbit looked up, its eyes filled with gratitude as it relaxed in their presence. Max felt a warmth in his heart, knowing he had shown compassion to someone in need.

As they continued their walk, Mira encouraged Max to think about times when he had felt sad, happy, or scared. "Empathy also means remembering our own experiences," Mira explained. "When we understand our own feelings, it becomes easier to relate to others who might be feeling the same way."

Max thought back to moments in his own journey, times when he had felt frustrated during his search or happy when his friends helped him. He realized that these emotions were things other animals might feel, too, and that empathy was about connecting with those shared experiences.

"I remember feeling frustrated when I couldn't find my mittens," Max said thoughtfully. "Maybe if someone else feels that way, I can understand them better and help them feel better, too."

Mira smiled, her gaze warm with pride. "Exactly, Max. Empathy lets us see others through a lens of understanding and kindness. It helps us remember that everyone has struggles, just like we do."

Max felt a sense of connection as he thought about the shared experiences of his friends. He realized that empathy was a way to bridge the gap between himself and others, creating a sense of unity and compassion.

Next, Mira suggested an exercise to help Max practice empathy actively. She led him to a small pond, where they watched the reflection of the trees and sky in the still water.

"Empathy is like this pond, Max," Mira explained. "When we connect with others, we become a mirror, reflecting their feelings and experiences back to them. Let's practice by thinking about some of your friends and imagining how they might feel in different situations."

Max thought for a moment and chose his friend Tully. "I remember when Tully felt nervous about a game. He wasn't sure he'd be able to keep up, and he looked really worried."

Mira nodded. "How do you think you could show empathy to Tully in that moment?"

Max considered her question carefully. "I could let him know that it's okay to feel nervous and remind him that we're all here to support him. Maybe I could even stay by his side during the game so he feels less alone."

Mira's eyes softened with pride. "That's beautiful, Max. By imagining how Tully feels, you're able to offer him the understanding and comfort he needs. That's the heart of empathy—being there for others in a way that respects their feelings."

Max felt a deep sense of fulfillment as he realized how powerful empathy could be. He understood that it was about more than just comforting others; it was about connecting with them in a way that made them feel truly understood.

Mira suggested that Max think of someone who had helped him recently and express his gratitude in an empathetic way. Max immediately thought of his mom, who had been there for him every step of the way, encouraging him and listening to his worries.

"Empathy also means recognizing the kindness of others and showing appreciation for it," Mira said gently. "When you thank someone with empathy, you acknowledge the effort and love they've shown."

Max decided he would thank his mom by telling her how much her support had meant to him during his search. He realized that by showing empathy in his gratitude, he could make his thanks even more meaningful.

Chapter 20: Patience in Reflection with Sage the Turtle

After his lesson on empathy with Mira, Max felt a new sense of connection to his friends and family. He had come to understand the importance of listening, understanding, and offering comfort. As he reflected on all he had learned, Max began to realize that he still felt a need for one last, important lesson. He wanted to better understand how to find peace in moments of waiting and to practice patience, not just as a skill for achieving goals, but as a way of being.

To learn more, he decided to visit Sage, the wise turtle who lived by the small pond near the edge of the schoolyard. Sage was known for his calm and steady nature, never rushing or showing frustration, even in the busiest of times. Max had often seen Sage sitting quietly by the water, reflecting peacefully, and he hoped Sage could show him how to find patience in a lasting way.

Max found Sage on a smooth rock by the pond, his shell gleaming softly in the sunlight. Sage seemed to be simply observing the world around him, his eyes gentle and thoughtful.

"Hello, Sage," Max said softly, not wanting to interrupt the calm.

Sage looked over at Max and nodded with a serene smile. "Hello, Max. What a pleasant surprise. How can I help you today?"

Max took a deep breath, feeling at ease in Sage's calming presence. "I've learned so much from everyone about patience, perseverance, and resilience. But I want to understand how to be patient on a deeper level. I want to feel calm inside, even when I have to wait or things don't go my way. Can you teach me?"

Sage nodded slowly, his gaze thoughtful. "Ah, Max, patience is indeed a lifelong practice. True patience is about finding peace within yourself, allowing time to flow naturally and embracing each moment as it comes. Come, let's sit by the pond, and I'll show you a few ways to deepen your patience."

Max settled down beside Sage, eager to learn from the gentle turtle's wisdom.

Sage began by introducing Max to the idea of mindful observation. He encouraged Max to focus on his surroundings, observing each detail slowly and carefully. "When we are truly present, patience becomes easier. Watch the water, Max. Notice how it moves calmly, even when the breeze stirs the surface."

Max gazed at the pond, watching as gentle ripples spread across the water's surface. He noticed how each ripple moved slowly, gracefully, without rushing. Sage guided him to follow each ripple with his eyes, appreciating its movement and taking in the beauty of the pond.

"Patience is about slowing down and appreciating what's in front of you," Sage explained softly. "When we learn to observe without hurry, we feel more connected to the world, and time doesn't feel so pressing."

Max took a deep breath, feeling the calm of the pond settle within him. For the first time, he understood that patience was not just about waiting—it was about being fully present in the moment and finding peace in the act of observing.

Next, Sage introduced Max to the idea of acceptance. He explained that sometimes, impatience came from resisting things that couldn't be changed, like waiting for something or dealing with uncertainty. "Patience grows stronger when we learn to accept what we cannot control," Sage said, his voice soft and steady. "Try closing your eyes, Max, and imagine yourself in a place where you must wait. Rather than feeling frustrated, focus on accepting the moment for what it is."

Max closed his eyes, imagining himself waiting for his mittens during his search. At first, he felt a familiar urge to move quickly, to solve the problem right away. But as he breathed deeply, he practiced accepting the moment, allowing himself to feel at peace even without an immediate solution.

Sage continued, "Acceptance is about letting go of the need for things to be different. When we accept each moment as it is, we find calm, even when there is uncertainty."

Max opened his eyes, feeling a sense of release. He realized that patience was more than just a skill—it was an inner peace that allowed him to embrace each moment, whether it brought answers or simply asked him to wait.

Afterward, Sage suggested a practice in stillness. He led Max to a quiet patch of grass near the pond, where they could sit together without distractions. "Being still is one of the most powerful ways to build patience," Sage explained. "In stillness, we learn to be comfortable with ourselves, without needing constant movement or answers."

They sat quietly, side by side, listening to the sounds of nature. The birds chirped softly in the trees, and a gentle breeze rustled the leaves. Max closed his eyes, feeling the coolness of the grass and the warmth of the sun. The stillness around him brought a deep sense of peace, and he felt his mind calm as he focused on simply being in the moment.

As they sat, Sage spoke softly, sharing his wisdom. "True patience is found in the quiet spaces within ourselves. It's a willingness to let go of the need for everything to happen right away and to trust that all things come in their own time."

Max let Sage's words sink in, feeling the truth of his advice. In the quietness, he felt a sense of connection to the world, realizing that patience was about more than waiting—it was about finding peace within and embracing the rhythm of life.

Chapter 21: Forgiveness with Ember the Crow

Max's journey of learning had brought him a long way from where he had started. Each lesson from his friends and family had enriched him, filling his heart with values he knew he would carry forever. But even as he grew wiser, Max felt a tug of unfinished business. He thought back to the day he had lost his mittens and remembered the moment he had scolded himself for being careless. Though he'd found his mittens and learned so much along the way, he still felt a hint of guilt, a small voice in his mind that reminded him of his mistake.

Max realized that there was one last lesson he needed: forgiveness, not just for others, but also for himself. To learn more, he decided to visit Ember, the intelligent and kind-hearted crow who was known for her understanding nature. Ember had helped others overcome their own mistakes and find peace, and Max hoped she could help him let go of his lingering guilt.

Max found Ember perched in her favorite tree near the schoolyard, her feathers gleaming black in the sunlight. She was observing her surroundings with a thoughtful gaze, her sharp eyes taking in every detail.

"Hello, Ember," Max greeted her, looking up at the wise crow. "Can I talk to you about something?"

Ember tilted her head, giving him a gentle smile. "Of course, Max. I'm always here to listen. What's on your mind?"

Max took a deep breath, feeling a mix of relief and nervousness. "I've learned so much from everyone, and I'm really grateful. But I still feel guilty about losing my mittens in the first place. I know it was an accident, but part of me keeps feeling bad about it. I thought maybe you could help me understand how to forgive myself."

Ember's eyes softened with empathy. "Ah, Max, forgiveness is a powerful way to bring peace to our hearts. Forgiving ourselves is often harder than forgiving others, but it's one of the most important things we can learn. Let's explore a few ways to practice forgiveness, starting with understanding why we feel the way we do."

Max nodded, feeling comforted by Ember's gentle words. He realized that his journey wasn't just about learning values—it was also about finding inner peace.

Ember began by helping Max reflect on his feelings without judgment. She encouraged him to think back to the day he had lost his mittens and to remember how he had felt in that moment. "Try to see yourself through kind eyes, Max," she said softly. "Imagine you're watching a friend who made a mistake. Would you be harsh, or would you offer understanding?"

Max closed his eyes, picturing himself on the day he had lost his mittens. He remembered the excitement of playing with Tully, the laughter and fun they'd shared. Then he saw himself searching frantically, feeling the first pangs of guilt and worry. He imagined how he would feel if it were Tully in his place, and he realized that he would tell his friend it was okay—that everyone makes mistakes.

"I think I'd tell Tully not to be so hard on himself," Max said thoughtfully. "I'd remind him that it was just an accident."

Ember nodded approvingly. "That's exactly right, Max. Forgiveness begins with kindness. When we see ourselves through compassionate eyes, it becomes easier to let go of guilt."

Max opened his eyes, feeling a small weight lift from his heart. He realized that forgiving himself might be about treating himself with the same understanding he offered others.

Next, Ember introduced Max to the idea of learning from mistakes as a way of practicing self-forgiveness. "When we learn from our mistakes, they become lessons rather than regrets," Ember explained.

"Think about everything you've gained from this journey. If you hadn't lost your mittens, you might not have had the chance to learn so much."

Max thought about this, remembering each lesson he had learned from his friends. He had discovered patience, gratitude, empathy, and resilience—all because of that small mistake. He began to see that his journey had been filled with gifts he wouldn't have received if everything had gone perfectly.

"I guess losing my mittens helped me grow in ways I didn't expect," Max said, smiling softly. "I wouldn't change that, even if I could."

Ember's eyes sparkled with pride. "Exactly, Max. Mistakes are part of being human, and each one gives us a chance to learn something valuable. When we learn from our mistakes, they become part of our growth, helping us become wiser and more understanding."

Max felt a sense of acceptance as he reflected on his journey. He realized that his mistake hadn't made him less; it had helped him become more.

Ember then encouraged Max to practice letting go. She guided him to find a small pebble and hold it in his hand. "Imagine this pebble is your guilt, Max," she said gently. "Sometimes, we carry guilt like this, holding onto it tightly even when it weighs us down. But true forgiveness means letting go, allowing ourselves to move forward with a light heart."

Max held the pebble, feeling its weight in his hand. He thought about how he had carried guilt over his mistake, how he had held onto the feeling even after finding his mittens and learning so much. Slowly, he walked to the edge of the pond, and with a deep breath, he released the pebble into the water.

As the pebble sank beneath the surface, Max felt a wave of relief wash over him. It was as if he had finally let go of the guilt, freeing himself to embrace the lessons he had learned.

Ember watched him with a gentle smile. "Forgiveness is a release, Max. When we let go of guilt, we make room for peace and understanding. Carrying guilt doesn't make us stronger; letting it go does."

Max nodded, feeling lighter than he had in a long time. He realized that forgiveness wasn't about ignoring his mistake—it was about accepting it, learning from it, and allowing himself to move forward without regret.

Ember advised Max to think of a way to celebrate his journey. "Forgiveness also means honoring your growth, Max," she said softly. "Think about everything you've learned and how it has shaped you. Celebrate the person you've become, not in spite of your mistakes but because of them."

Max decided he would write a letter to himself, listing each lesson he had learned from his friends and family, and expressing his gratitude for his journey. He knew that this letter would remind him of the importance of kindness, patience, and forgiveness whenever he felt uncertain.

Chapter 22: Humility with Ezra the Snail

After his lesson on forgiveness with Ember, Max felt as though he had come full circle in his journey. Each friend had given him wisdom, helping him grow in ways he had never imagined. But as he reflected on everything he had learned, Max realized there was still one more value he wanted to understand: humility.

Humility, Max remembered, was about being modest and respectful, recognizing that we all have strengths and weaknesses. Max wanted to learn how to stay grounded, even with everything he had accomplished. He knew that humility would help him appreciate the contributions of others and avoid becoming overly focused on his own successes.

To explore humility, Max decided to visit Ezra, a gentle and thoughtful snail who was known for his calm and modest nature. Ezra always moved at his own pace, never rushing, and he seemed genuinely content with who he was. Max admired Ezra's quiet confidence and hoped he could learn how to carry his achievements with grace.

Max found Ezra in the school garden, slowly making his way along the edge of a flowerbed. Ezra looked up as Max approached, his calm eyes bright with welcome.

"Hello, Ezra," Max said, bending down to speak with his friend. "I was hoping you could teach me about humility. I've learned so much, and I feel really proud of what I've accomplished. But I want to make sure I stay grounded and remember that my friends helped me get here."

Ezra smiled softly, his antennae twitching in acknowledgment. "Ah, humility is indeed a valuable lesson, Max. It's about remembering that we are all part of something bigger. Humility helps us stay connected to others, showing respect for their contributions and understanding our place in the world. I would be honored to share what I know."

Max smiled, feeling a sense of calm in Ezra's presence. He knew he was about to learn something meaningful.

Ezra began by guiding Max through an exercise in appreciating smallness. He encouraged Max to lie down beside the flowerbed and look closely at the tiny details around them: the delicate petals, the small veins in the leaves, and the tiny insects moving quietly through the plants.

"Humility starts with understanding that even the smallest things have value," Ezra explained softly. "Every leaf, every flower, and every creature plays an important role in the world. By appreciating the small things, we recognize that greatness isn't just in what's big or visible—it's also in the quiet, everyday contributions."

Max looked closely at a tiny beetle crawling along a leaf, noticing the shimmer of its shell in the sunlight. He saw the small web of a spider, glistening with dew, and marveled at the intricate beauty in each detail. Ezra's words helped him realize that humility meant appreciating these small wonders without needing them to be grand or impressive.

"Humility teaches us to find beauty in the small things," Ezra continued. "When we see the world with this mindset, we become more connected, more respectful, and more willing to listen."

Max nodded, feeling a new sense of admiration for the quiet details around him. He understood that humility was about seeing the value in everything, not just the things that stood out.

Next, Ezra encouraged Max to reflect on his journey, not by focusing on his achievements but by remembering everyone who had helped him along the way. He suggested that Max close his eyes and picture each friend who had shared a lesson or offered support.

"Humility also means acknowledging that we don't succeed alone," Ezra explained gently. "Think about each person who contributed to your growth. They each had a part in helping you become who you are."

Max thought of Tully's patience, Rina's organization, Piper's positivity, and all the friends who had guided him. He felt a surge of gratitude as he remembered how each friend had contributed something unique to his journey. With Ezra's encouragement, he realized that his achievements were not just his own; they were woven from the kindness and wisdom of those who had supported him.

"I couldn't have done it alone," Max said softly, feeling a renewed sense of respect for his friends. "Each friend taught me something valuable. I wouldn't be who I am without them."

Ezra nodded approvingly. "Exactly, Max. Humility is about seeing ourselves as part of a larger story, one where everyone has a role. When we remember this, we carry our successes with gratitude and respect, rather than pride."

Max felt a sense of warmth in his heart. He understood that humility was about honoring the contributions of others and recognizing that his journey had been a shared one.

To help Max further understand humility, Ezra introduced him to the idea of quietness. He suggested that Max spend a few moments simply being still, observing the world without needing to speak or act.

"Humility also means knowing when to be quiet," Ezra explained. "In stillness, we learn to listen, to observe, and to appreciate the world around us without needing to take center stage."

Max sat quietly beside Ezra, watching the gentle sway of the flowers in the breeze and the soft hum of bees moving from bloom to bloom. He noticed how each creature went about its own task, each playing a small but essential role. Max felt humbled by the beauty and simplicity of nature, realizing that he didn't need to be the focus—he could simply be part of something larger.

Ezra's quiet presence beside him helped Max feel connected to the world in a new way. He understood that humility was not about making himself smaller but about embracing his place within a vast, interconnected world.

"Sometimes, humility is as simple as stepping back and observing," Ezra said softly. "When we let go of the need to be noticed, we open ourselves to the beauty of everything around us."

Chapter 23: Perseverance with Gia the Honeybee

Max's journey through learning had given him an appreciation for patience, humility, forgiveness, and so many other values that had filled his heart with joy. He knew each lesson was a treasure that he would carry forever. Yet, as he reflected on his experiences, he realized there was one more quality he wanted to strengthen: perseverance.

Perseverance, he understood, was about continuing on, no matter how tough things got, and he knew it was a skill that would help him through any challenge life might bring. For this lesson, Max decided to visit Gia, a diligent and resilient honeybee known for her incredible work ethic and dedication. Gia spent her days collecting nectar and pollen, always buzzing from one flower to the next with tireless energy.

After school, Max found Gia near the garden, hovering around a cluster of bright flowers. She moved from bloom to bloom, carefully gathering pollen and nectar with precision. Gia noticed Max approaching and greeted him with a cheerful hum.

"Hello, Max! What brings you to the garden today?" Gia asked, pausing her work to rest on a nearby petal.

Max smiled, feeling admiration for Gia's dedication. "I wanted to talk to you about perseverance. I've learned a lot on my journey, but I think I could use some help with staying determined, especially when things get hard. You always work so steadily, and I'd love to learn from you."

Gia's wings buzzed with excitement as she nodded. "Oh, perseverance is something I know all about, Max! It's about sticking to a task, no matter how long it takes. I'd be delighted to share what I know with you. Come along, and I'll show you what it means to keep going, one step at a time."

Max felt a thrill of anticipation as he followed Gia through the garden, eager to learn from her unwavering spirit.

Gia began by showing Max the process of collecting nectar and pollen. She explained that while each flower only provided a small amount, every tiny contribution mattered in the end.

"Perseverance is about focusing on the small steps," Gia said as she carefully gathered pollen from a daisy. "If I looked at the whole garden and thought about collecting from every flower, it might feel overwhelming. But by taking it one flower at a time, I can stay focused and keep going."

Max watched as Gia moved from one flower to the next with grace and precision. He realized that she was teaching him a valuable lesson: when faced with a big challenge, breaking it down into small, manageable steps made it easier to persevere.

Max picked up a small pebble and imagined it as a flower, following Gia's lead by pretending to collect nectar. With each "flower," he told himself he was one step closer to reaching his goal. The exercise helped him feel calm and focused, even as he imagined a garden full of challenges.

"I see what you mean, Gia," Max said thoughtfully. "When I focus on each small step, the big task doesn't seem as hard. It's like building patience while staying determined."

Gia nodded, her wings buzzing in agreement. "Exactly, Max! Perseverance is about having patience with the process and trusting that each little step brings you closer to your goal."

Next, Gia introduced Max to the importance of resilience in perseverance. She led him to a patch of flowers that was farther from the garden, requiring a longer journey and more effort to reach.

"Sometimes, perseverance means facing obstacles along the way," Gia explained. "There are days when the weather changes, or the flowers are harder to reach, but I still push on, knowing that every effort counts. Resilience helps me keep going, even when it's tough."

Max followed Gia to the distant flowers, feeling the extra effort it took to reach them. He understood that perseverance wasn't just about moving forward—it was about handling setbacks and challenges with strength. Each step he took became a lesson in resilience, reminding him that perseverance meant facing challenges without giving up.

As they reached the flowers, Max felt a surge of satisfaction. He realized that overcoming the extra effort made the achievement feel even more rewarding.

"Thank you for showing me this, Gia," Max said, smiling at her. "I see now that perseverance is also about resilience, about not giving up when things get difficult."

Gia's eyes sparkled with pride. "You've got it, Max. Perseverance means continuing, even when the path isn't easy. Resilience is what makes it possible to keep going, no matter the obstacles."

Afterward, Gia led Max back toward the garden and shared another part of perseverance: consistency. She explained that gathering pollen and nectar wasn't just something she did once—it was something she repeated every day, knowing that each effort added up over time.

"Perseverance isn't about doing something perfectly once; it's about doing it consistently," Gia said as she moved to another flower. "Each day, I come here and gather pollen and nectar. It may seem small, but when I do it over and over, it makes a big difference."

Max thought about this lesson, realizing that consistency was key to achieving long-term goals. He remembered how he had searched for his mittens day after day, even when he didn't find them right away. By sticking with his search, he had eventually succeeded.

Chapter 24: Honesty with Bosco the Hedgehog

As Max's journey neared its end, he felt filled with gratitude for all the values and skills he had gained along the way. He'd learned about kindness, resilience, patience, and countless other virtues that had helped him grow. Yet, as he reflected on each lesson, he realized there was one more quality he needed to revisit: honesty.

Max had practiced honesty when he admitted to his mom and Mr. Ponder that he had lost his mittens, but he wanted to understand it more deeply. He knew that honesty wasn't just about telling the truth—it was also about being open with himself and others, even when it felt difficult. For guidance on this final value, Max decided to visit Bosco, a wise and thoughtful hedgehog known for his straightforward nature and his commitment to honesty.

Max found Bosco near the school's stone wall, where the hedgehog was collecting small stones and arranging them in neat rows. Bosco looked up as Max approached, his expression warm and welcoming.

"Hello, Bosco," Max greeted him, feeling a sense of respect for his friend's thoughtful gaze. "I've been learning a lot on my journey, but I want to understand honesty better. You always seem so open and straightforward, and I'd like to learn from you."

Bosco smiled, his small eyes shining with approval. "Ah, Max, honesty is indeed a valuable quality. It's not just about telling the truth—it's about being true to yourself and others, even when it's challenging. I'd be happy to share what I know with you."

Max felt a sense of anticipation as he settled beside Bosco, eager to learn the true essence of honesty.

Bosco began by helping Max understand the importance of being honest with himself. He explained that honesty started with self-awareness, knowing how we truly feel and acknowledging it without hiding.

"Sometimes, we avoid being honest with ourselves because the truth can feel uncomfortable," Bosco said gently. "But when we face our feelings openly, we gain a clearer understanding of ourselves. Let's start by thinking about something that made you feel uncertain or uncomfortable."

Max thought back to the early days of his mitten search, remembering how he had felt embarrassed for losing them and worried about disappointing his mom. He realized that, deep down, he had tried to ignore these feelings, hoping they would go away on their own.

"I think I felt embarrassed when I first lost my mittens," Max admitted. "I was worried about what my friends and family would think, so I tried not to think about it too much."

Bosco nodded thoughtfully. "That's a good start, Max. Honesty with ourselves means accepting our feelings, even when they're uncomfortable. When we admit how we feel, we gain the power to face those feelings and move forward."

Max felt a sense of relief as he acknowledged his past embarrassment. He realized that being honest with himself had lifted a weight he hadn't noticed he was carrying. Bosco's guidance helped him see that honesty was a way of respecting his own emotions, allowing him to grow from them rather than hiding them away.

Next, Bosco encouraged Max to practice honesty in his relationships. He explained that honesty with others created trust, helping friends and family feel safe and valued.

"Honesty with others means being open about how you feel and what you need," Bosco said. "It's not always easy, but it helps build strong, meaningful connections. Think of a time when being honest with someone helped you understand each other better."

Max thought back to the time he had told his mom about losing his mittens. At first, he had been worried she would be disappointed, but her understanding had surprised him. Being honest had allowed them to work together, and he'd felt closer to her because of it.

"I remember feeling really nervous about telling my mom," Max admitted. "But being honest made me realize that she was there to help me, not to judge me."

Bosco smiled approvingly. "Exactly, Max. When we're honest with others, we give them the chance to understand and support us. It's a way of showing respect for their feelings, too, by trusting them enough to share openly."

Max felt grateful for Bosco's insight. He understood that honesty wasn't just a responsibility—it was a gift, one that allowed him to build trust and connection with the people he cared about.

To deepen Max's understanding of honesty, Bosco introduced him to the idea of gentle honesty, which involved speaking the truth kindly and thoughtfully. He explained that honesty didn't mean being harsh or hurtful; it was about sharing the truth in a way that respected others' feelings.

"Honesty should be balanced with kindness," Bosco said gently. "When we're honest, we should also consider how our words might affect others. Let's practice by imagining a situation where you need to tell someone something important, but you want to do it in a caring way."

Max thought about how he might tell Tully if he'd accidentally broken one of his toys. He realized that he could be honest while also being sensitive, acknowledging Tully's feelings and offering to help fix the toy.

"I think I'd tell Tully what happened and apologize for it," Max said thoughtfully. "But I'd also offer to help fix it, so he knows I care about making things right."

Bosco's eyes sparkled with pride. "That's a wonderful example, Max. Honesty means taking responsibility for our actions, but it also means approaching the truth with kindness. When we combine honesty with compassion, we strengthen our relationships."

Max felt a sense of peace as he considered Bosco's advice. He realized that honesty could be a way of showing care for others, building trust while also being thoughtful and respectful.

For their final exercise, Bosco encouraged Max to think about how he could continue practicing honesty in his daily life. He suggested that Max set a personal intention to be open and genuine in his interactions, making honesty a habit he could carry forward.

Chapter 25: Reflection and Farewell at the Friendship Gathering

The day had finally come for Max to gather his friends and family together for a special celebration. After his journey of growth, self-discovery, and learning, he wanted to express his gratitude to everyone who had helped him. Max planned a Friendship Gathering at the school playground, inviting each friend who had taught him something invaluable along the way. He was excited to share his reflections and honor the lessons that had shaped him into who he had become.

Max woke up early that morning, feeling a mixture of excitement and gratitude. He prepared a small speech and collected a few mementos from his journey, each one representing a lesson he'd learned. Max wanted to make sure everyone knew how much he valued their friendship and guidance.

By late morning, his friends started arriving one by one. Tully the turtle, Piper the rabbit, Rina the raccoon, Ollie the otter, and all his other friends gathered around, each one curious and touched by Max's invitation. Max's mom and a few teachers were there as well, watching with pride.

"Thank you all for coming," Max began, looking around at the group with a warm smile. "I wanted to gather everyone here to say thank you. Each of you taught me something special, and I feel so grateful to have such amazing friends and family."

The group settled in, smiling as Max took a deep breath and began to share the lessons he had learned.

Max started with Tully, the wise and patient turtle who had been one of the first friends to help him on his journey. He held up a small smooth stone he had picked up on their walk together.

"Tully taught me patience," Max said, smiling warmly at his friend. "You showed me that sometimes, the best way to solve a problem is to slow down, breathe, and take one step at a time. Thank you, Tully, for teaching me that patience makes the journey more enjoyable."

Tully nodded, his eyes warm with pride. "I'm glad I could help, Max. Patience is a wonderful companion on any journey."

Max continued, holding up a small, bright feather that reminded him of Piper's joyful spirit.

"Piper, you taught me positivity," he said with a grin. "Even when things were hard, you reminded me to look for the silver lining and keep my spirits high. Your positivity helped me stay hopeful, and I'll always remember that happiness is a choice we can make each day."

Piper beamed, her eyes shining with joy. "You're very welcome, Max! Happiness grows when we share it with others."

As he moved through each lesson, Max held up a small piece of string, representing the carefulness he had learned from Ollie. He held up a shiny pebble for Rina, a symbol of organization, and a tiny flower for Quinny, who had taught him teamwork. With each memento, he shared his gratitude, reflecting on how each friend had contributed something meaningful to his journey.

"Thank you, Ollie, for teaching me to pay attention to details," Max said, looking at the otter with a grateful smile. "Your carefulness helped me see the importance of being mindful in everything I do."

Ollie nodded, his smile gentle. "Being careful opens our eyes to all the small wonders around us, Max."

"And Rina, thank you for showing me the power of being organized," Max continued. "You helped me bring order to my search, and I'll always remember that planning makes every goal easier to reach."

Rina smiled with pride, giving Max an encouraging nod. "Being organized helps us bring our dreams to life, Max."

Max moved through each friend, expressing his gratitude with heartfelt words and meaningful gestures. He thanked Coach Bruno the bear for his encouragement, Mrs. Mallow the hare for teaching him the joy of helping others, and Rocky the badger for showing him resilience. Each friend smiled warmly, their hearts touched by Max's thoughtful reflections.

As he came to the final lessons, Max held up a leaf from the forest, representing the wisdom he had gained from Grandma Hazel. He looked toward his grandmother, his eyes filled with appreciation.

"Grandma, you taught me that sometimes, the answers we seek are already in our hearts," Max said softly. "Thank you for helping me see that wisdom grows when we take time to listen and reflect."

Grandma Hazel's eyes shone with love. "You've always had wisdom in your heart, Max. I'm so proud of the journey you've taken."

Max continued, thanking each friend who had taught him about forgiveness, humility, perseverance, and empathy. With each lesson, he felt his heart swell with gratitude, knowing that his journey would not have been the same without each person's guidance.

At the end of his speech, Max held up a small piece of fabric—a little patch from his mittens that had come loose over time. He looked around at the group, smiling as he held the fabric gently.

"These mittens were the reason I started this journey," Max said, his voice filled with emotion. "At first, I thought finding them was the most important thing. But along the way, I realized that what I was really finding was myself. Each of you helped me become who I am, and I wouldn't change any part of it. I am so grateful for each of you."

The group clapped and cheered, their hearts full of pride for Max. His friends gathered around him, each one offering words of encouragement, hugs, and smiles. Max felt surrounded by love, knowing that his journey had brought him closer to his friends and family in ways he had never imagined.

As the celebration continued, they shared stories, laughter, and warm snacks. Max felt a sense of fulfillment, knowing that he was supported by a community of people who cared about him deeply.

As the sun began to set, Max's mom gathered everyone for one final part of the celebration—a circle of reflection. Each friend took a moment to share a lesson they had learned from Max, expressing their admiration for his growth and determination.

Tully started, smiling at Max with pride. "Max, you taught me that patience grows even stronger when we share it with friends. I'm proud to know you."

One by one, each friend shared their reflections, thanking Max for his kindness, honesty, and courage. Max felt deeply touched, realizing that his journey had made a difference not only in his life but also in the lives of those around him.

When everyone had shared, Max's mom stepped forward, wrapping him in a warm hug. "Max, you've grown so much, and I am so proud of the person you're becoming. This journey was never just about finding your mittens—it was about finding your way in the world with kindness, courage, and love."

Max hugged her back, feeling tears of joy welling up in his eyes. He knew that his journey had changed him in ways that would stay with him forever, and he felt grateful for every lesson and every friend who had helped him along the way.

As the celebration drew to a close, Max looked around at the faces of his friends and family, feeling a deep sense of peace and gratitude. He knew that his journey was just beginning and that each value he had learned would guide him forward.

"Thank you all," Max said, his voice filled with warmth. "For being my friends, my family, and my guides. I'll carry each lesson with me, knowing that every moment has been a gift."

The group cheered one last time, their hearts full of love and pride for Max. As the stars began to twinkle in the evening sky, they said their goodbyes, each one carrying a piece of Max's journey in their hearts.

With that, Max's search for his mittens had come to a beautiful, fulfilling end. He had found not only what he was looking for but so much more—a community of love, wisdom, and unbreakable bonds.

Don't miss out!

Visit the website below and you can sign up to receive emails whenever Eric Gale publishes a new book. There's no charge and no obligation.

https://books2read.com/r/B-A-LKCVC-IZJIF

BOOKS 2 READ

Connecting independent readers to independent writers.

Did you love *Max's Missing Mittens*? Then you should read *Leo and the Leaf Pile*[1] by Nora Black!

In *Leo and the Leaf Pile,* Leo and his friends discover that life's greatest treasures lie in the beauty of shared experiences, kindness, and lasting friendship.

When Leo builds the biggest leaf pile in the Valley of Echoes, he invites his friends to join, creating moments filled with laughter, exploration, and heartwarming lessons on compassion. Through playful games, shared adventures, and thoughtful gestures, the friends learn the joy of welcoming others and appreciating the little wonders around them.

Leo and the Leaf Pile is a celebration of friendship, reminding readers that love and kindness make every moment brighter.

---

1. https://books2read.com/u/4AlaaJ
2. https://books2read.com/u/4AlaaJ

About the Publisher

Lightwave Publishers is dedicated to creating a world of wonder, learning, and imagination for young readers. Specializing in educative and captivating children's books, our mission is to inspire curiosity, foster creativity, and instill positive values. From heartwarming tales of friendship to adventures that teach diversity, inclusion, and resilience, our stories are crafted to entertain while nurturing critical thinking and emotional growth. Each book is thoughtfully designed to engage children aged 5 to 12, featuring vibrant illustrations and relatable characters. At Lightwave Publishers, we believe in the transformative power of stories to enlighten young minds and empower them to dream big.